YOU ARE HERE

WHITI HEREAKA
and
PEATA LARKIN

MASSEY UNIVERSITY PRESS

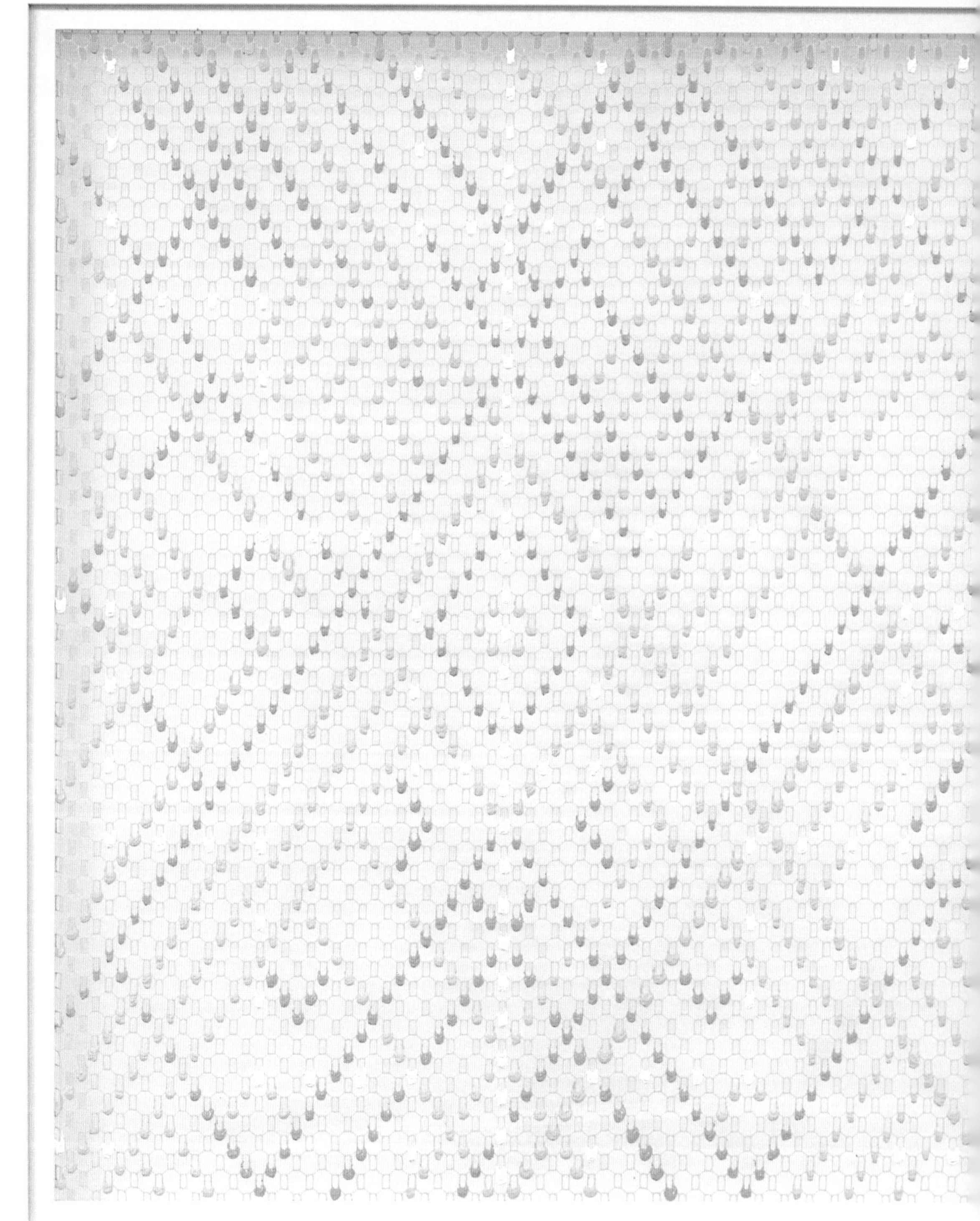

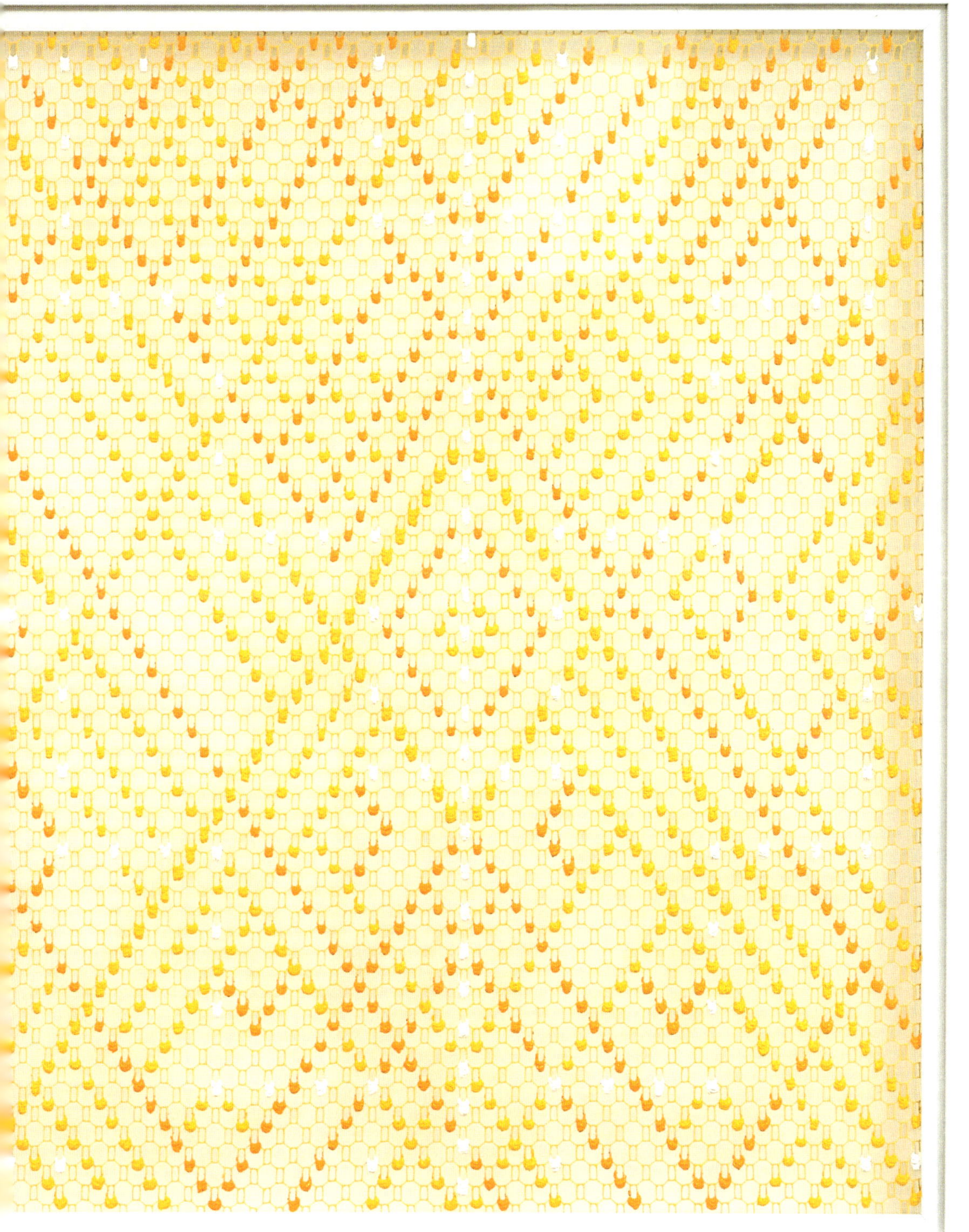

You are here.

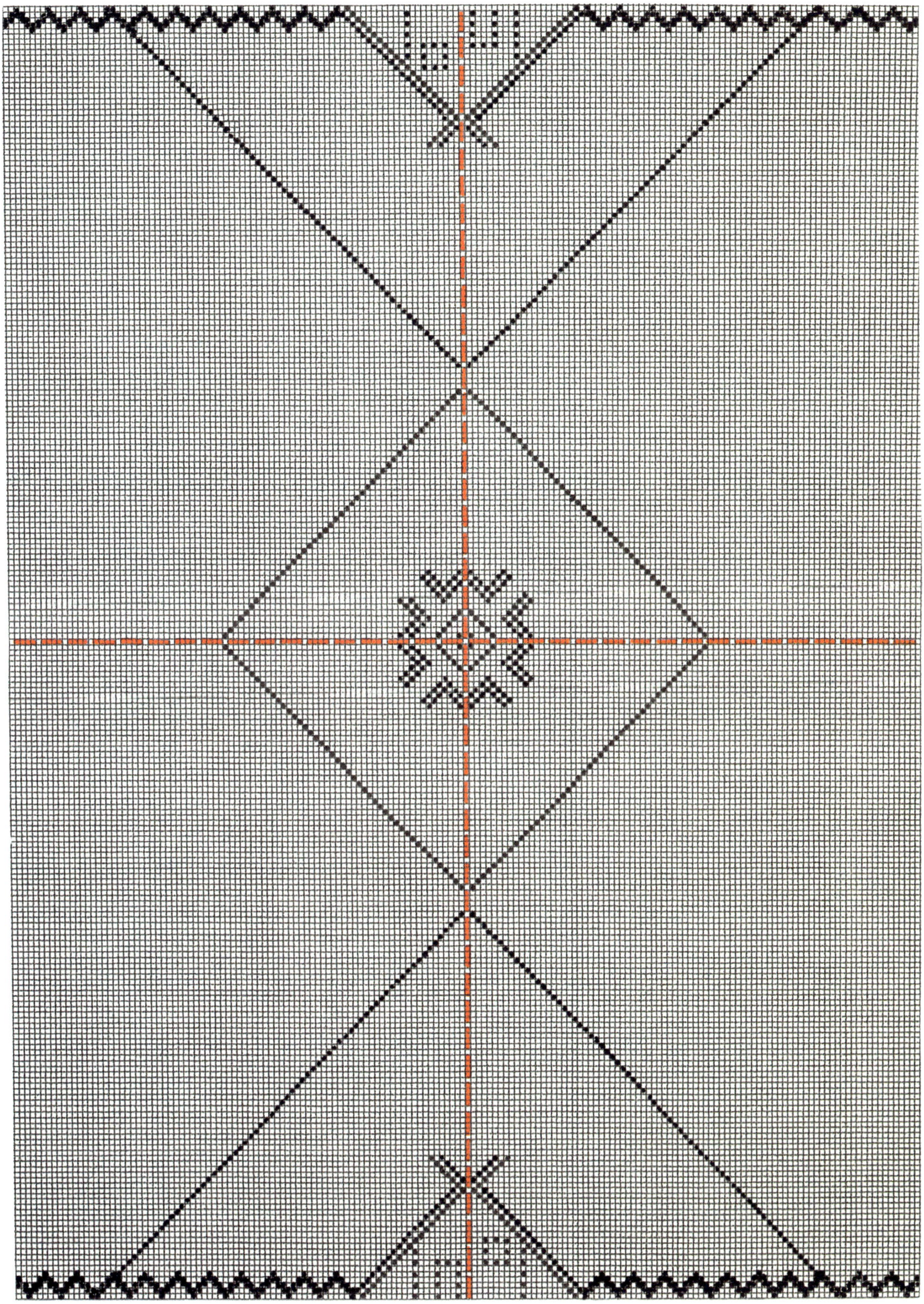

Back at the beginning again.

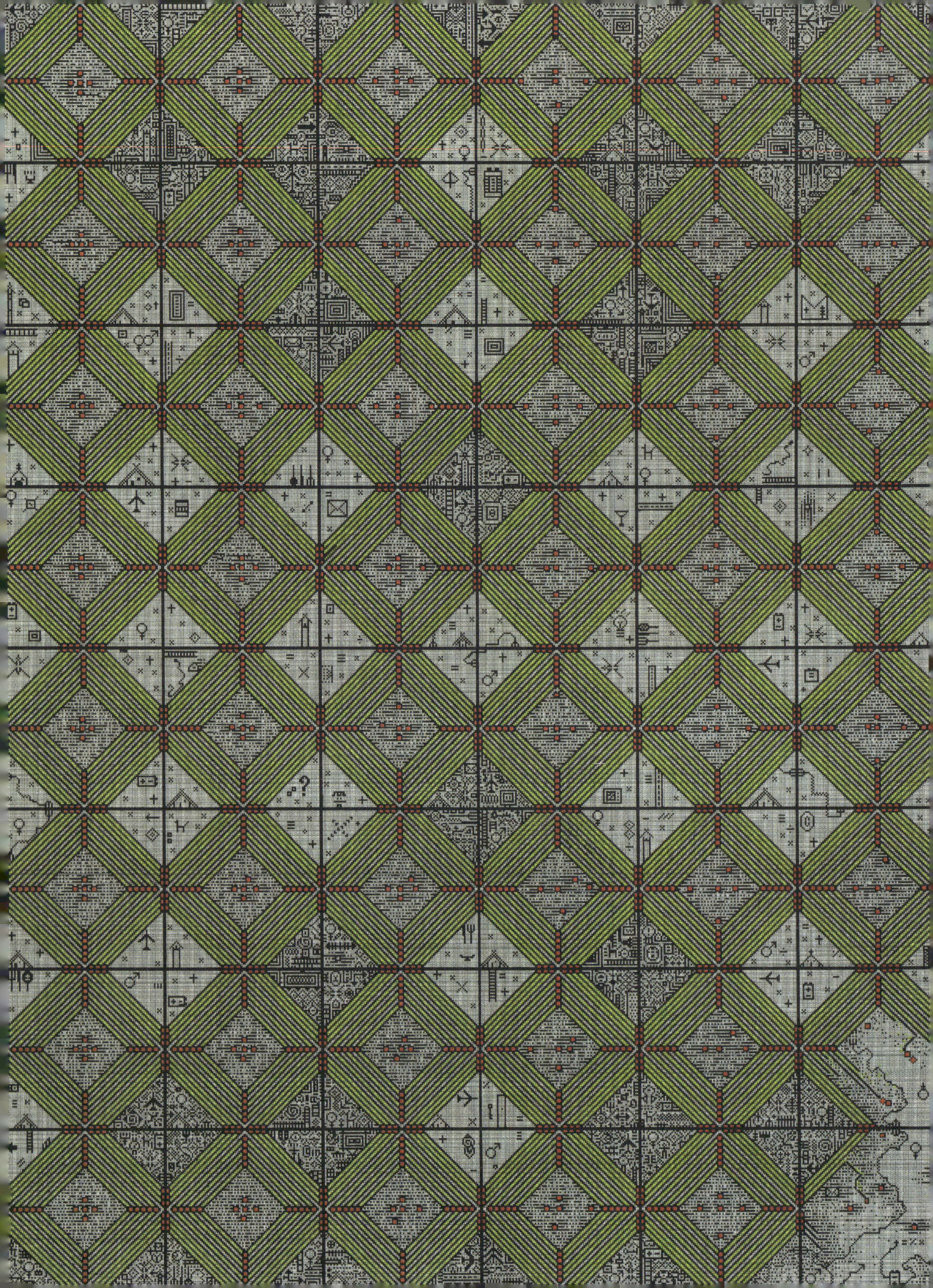

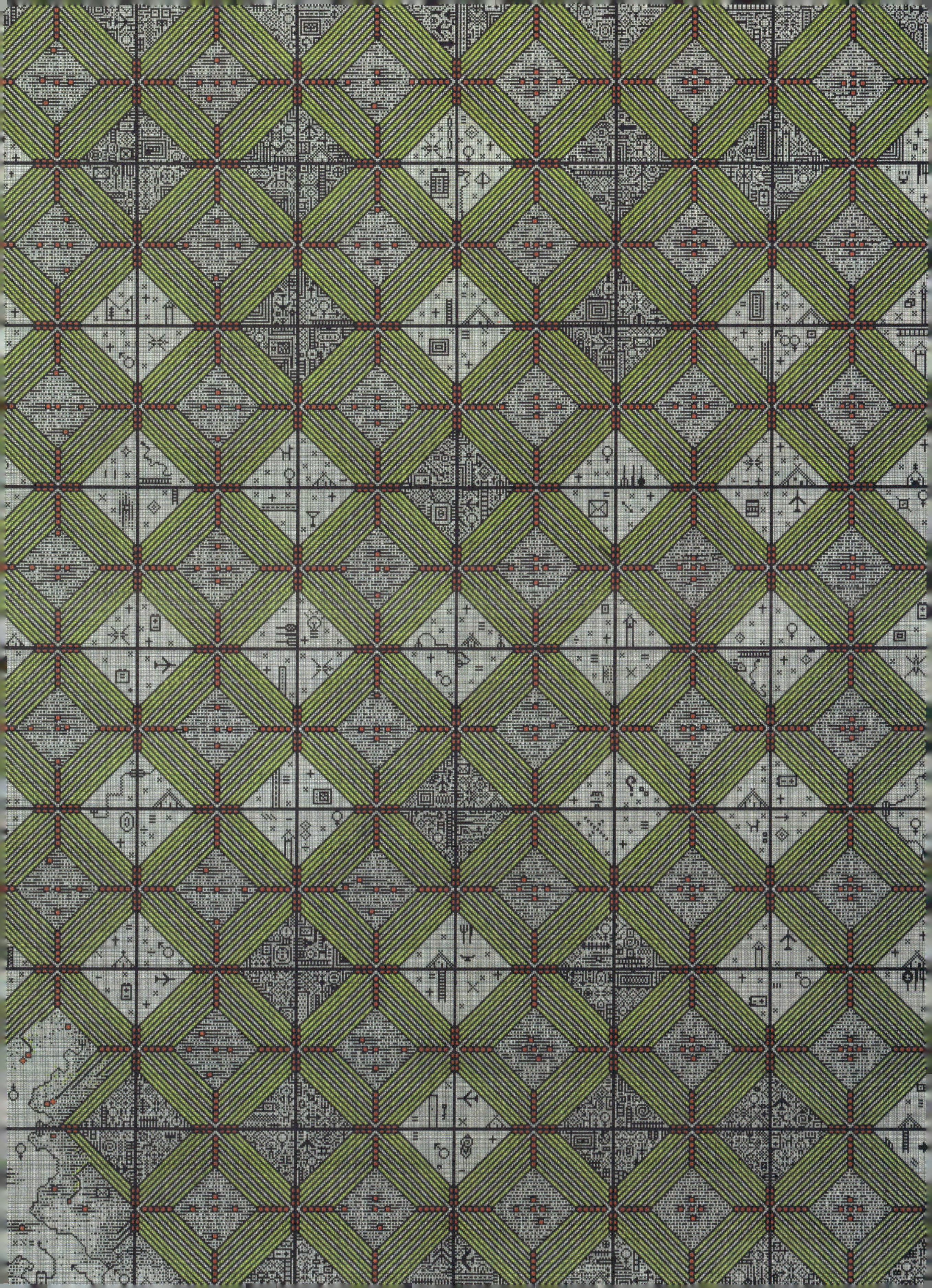

The beginning, yes, but not where you started.

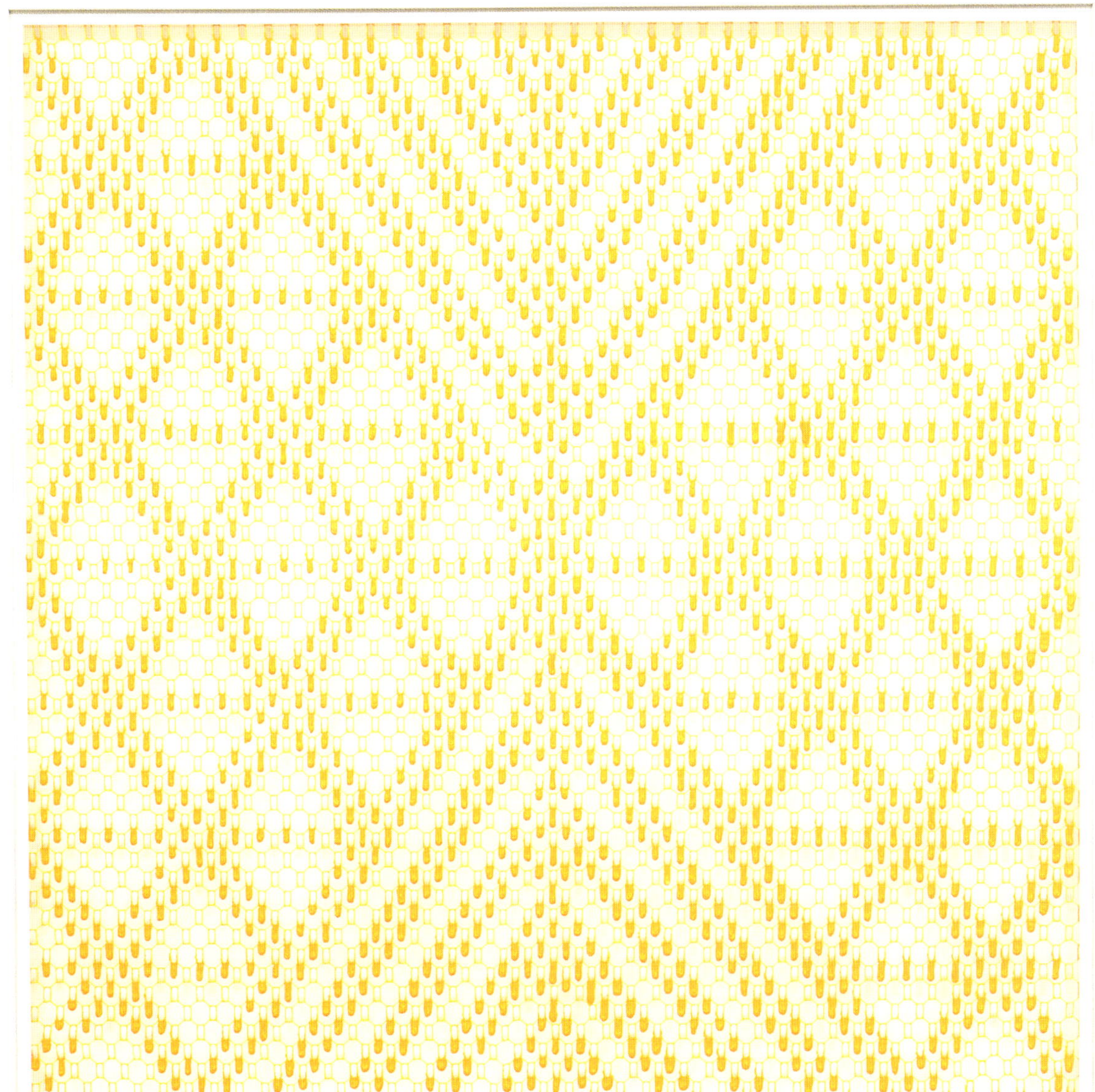

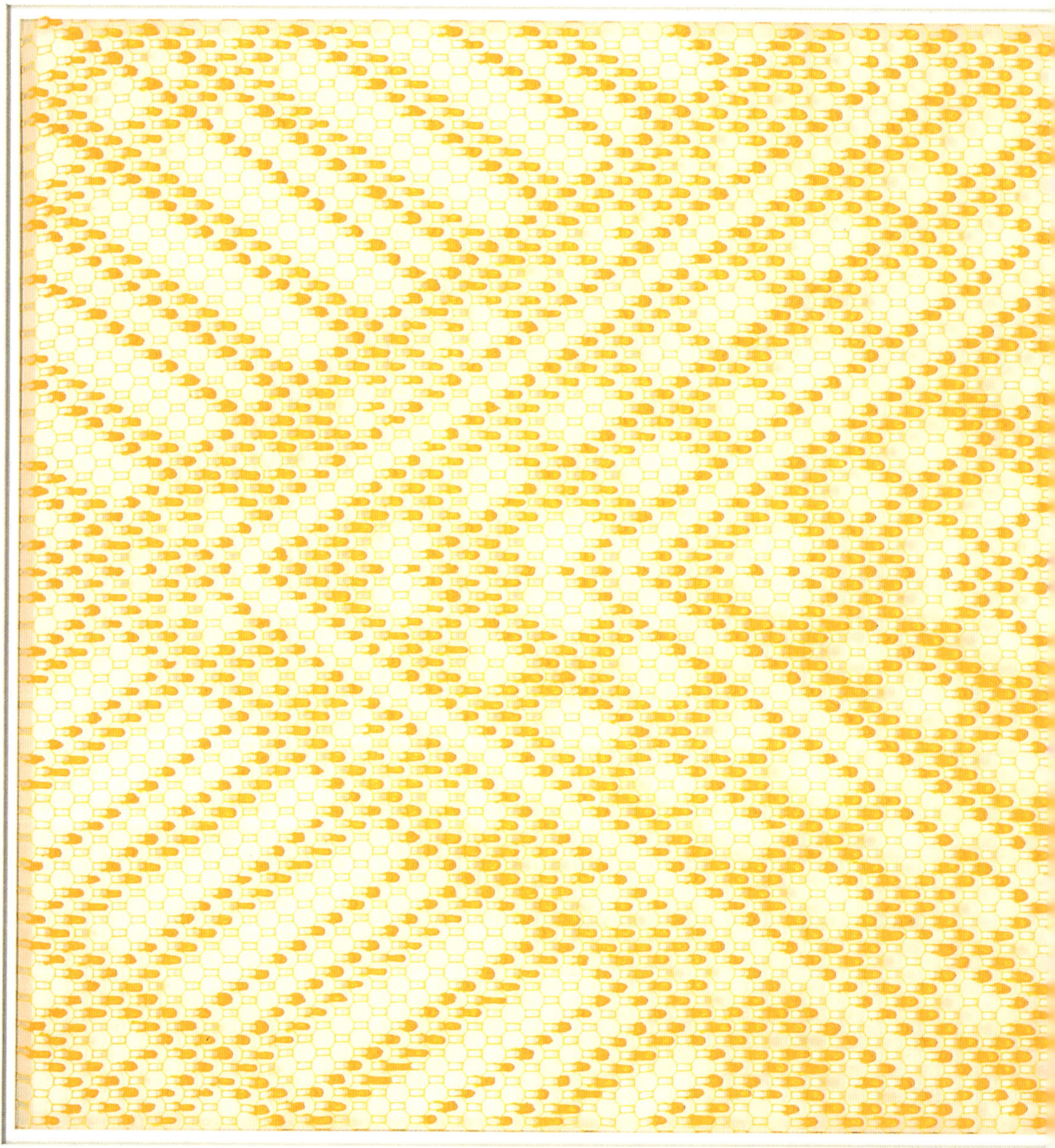

Not that long ago this would have worried you — to be beginning again.

Being back felt like losing ground, and it frustrated you to waste that time — blind to how far you had shifted.

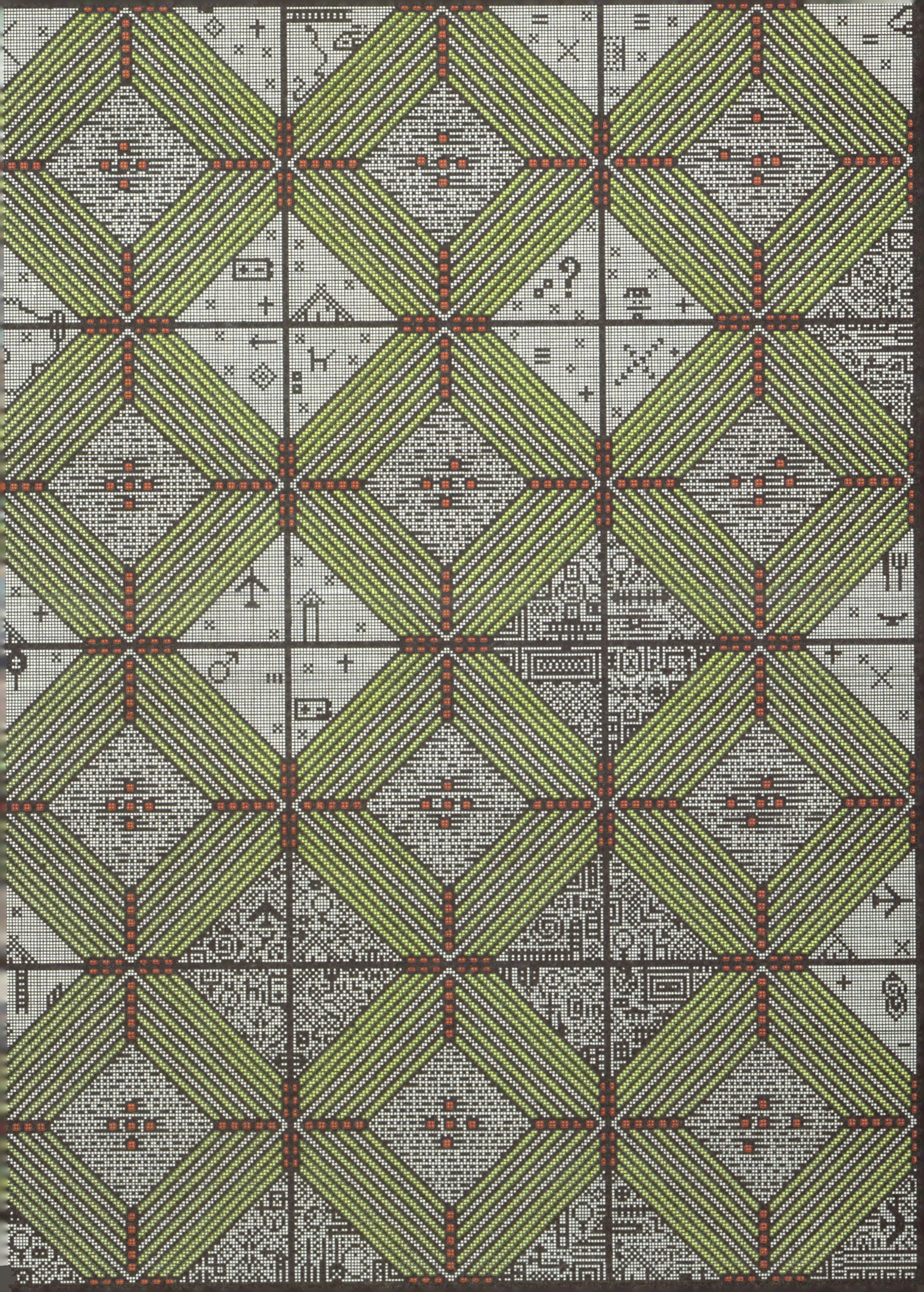

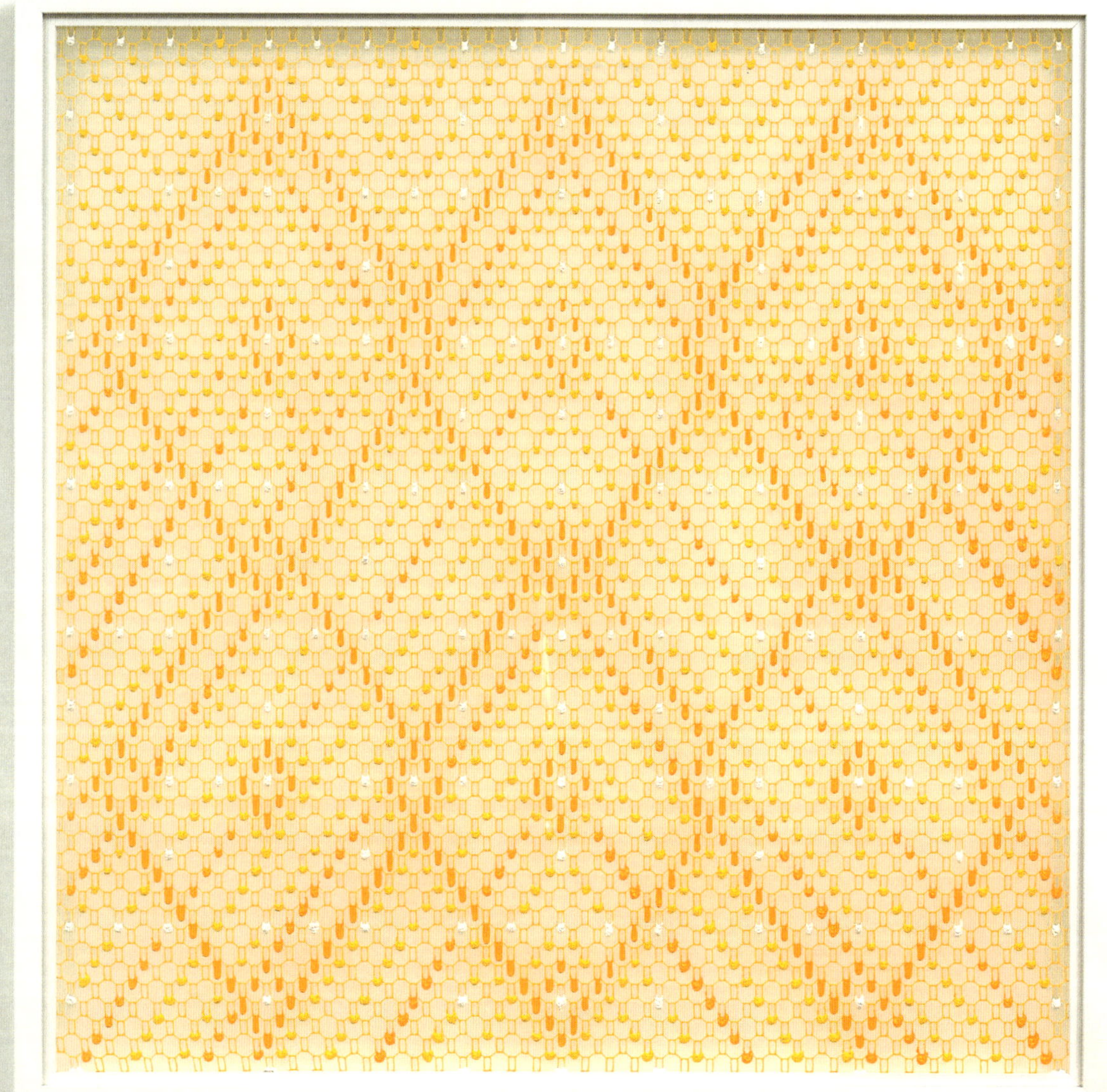

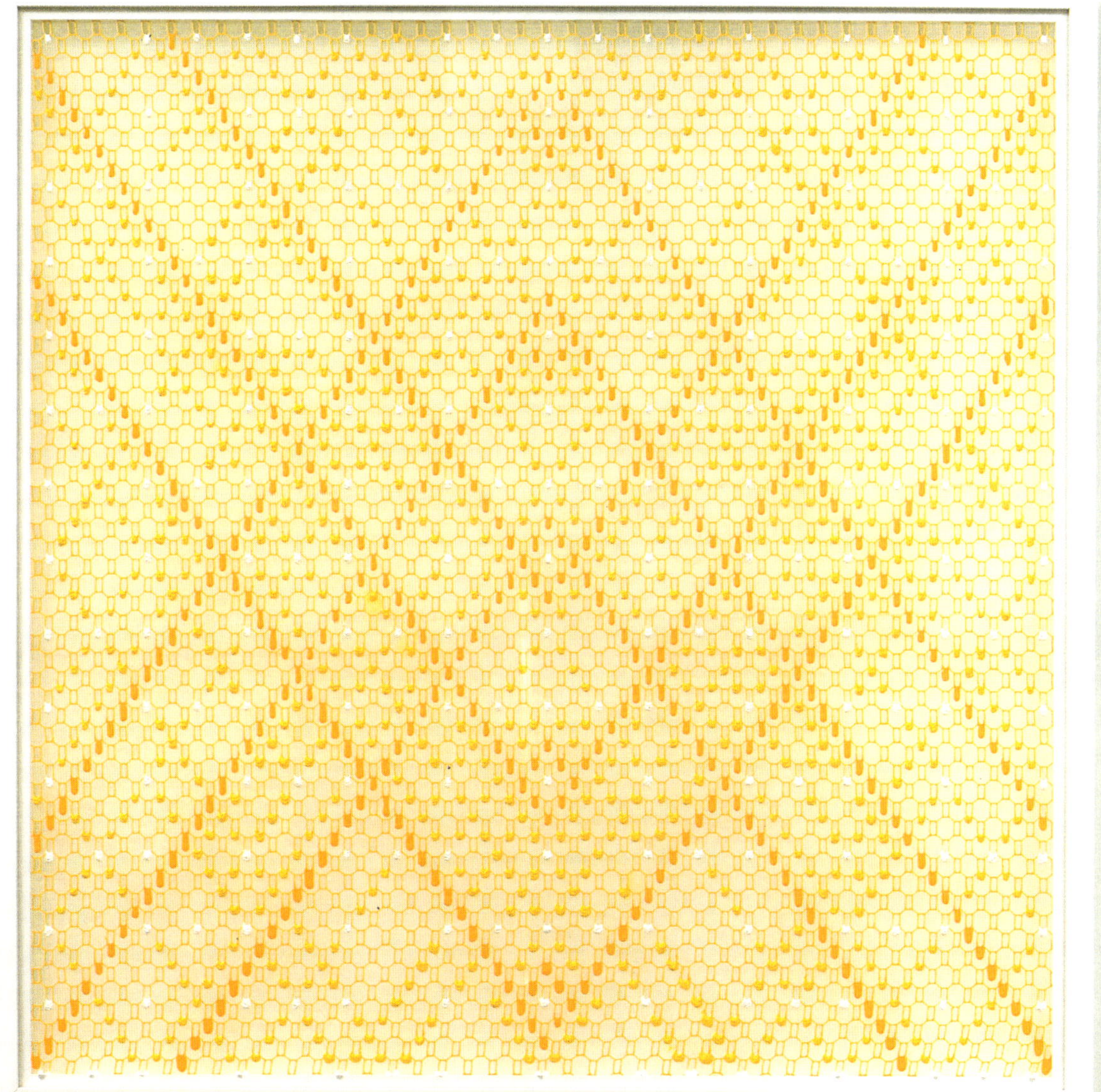

Although you recognise each other, you and this place have both changed. You are here at the beginning but not where you started. How long has it been? Do you count minutes, days, years?

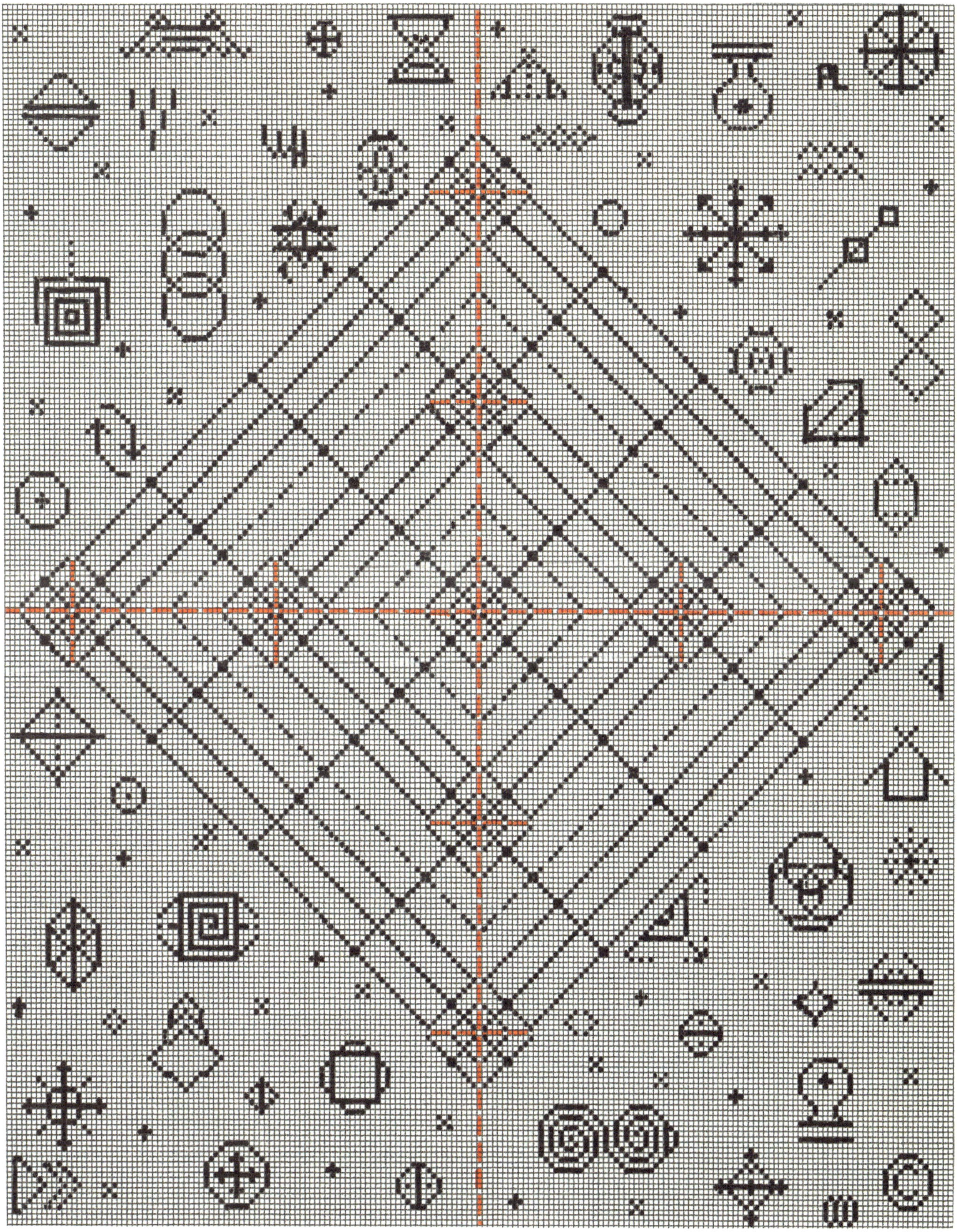

You left this place a while ago, but it has never really left you. Its mark is indelible on you; it shapes your thoughts and language, it colours everywhere else you have been. Even when you do not mean to, you compare every new home to this one, your first home, perhaps your only home.

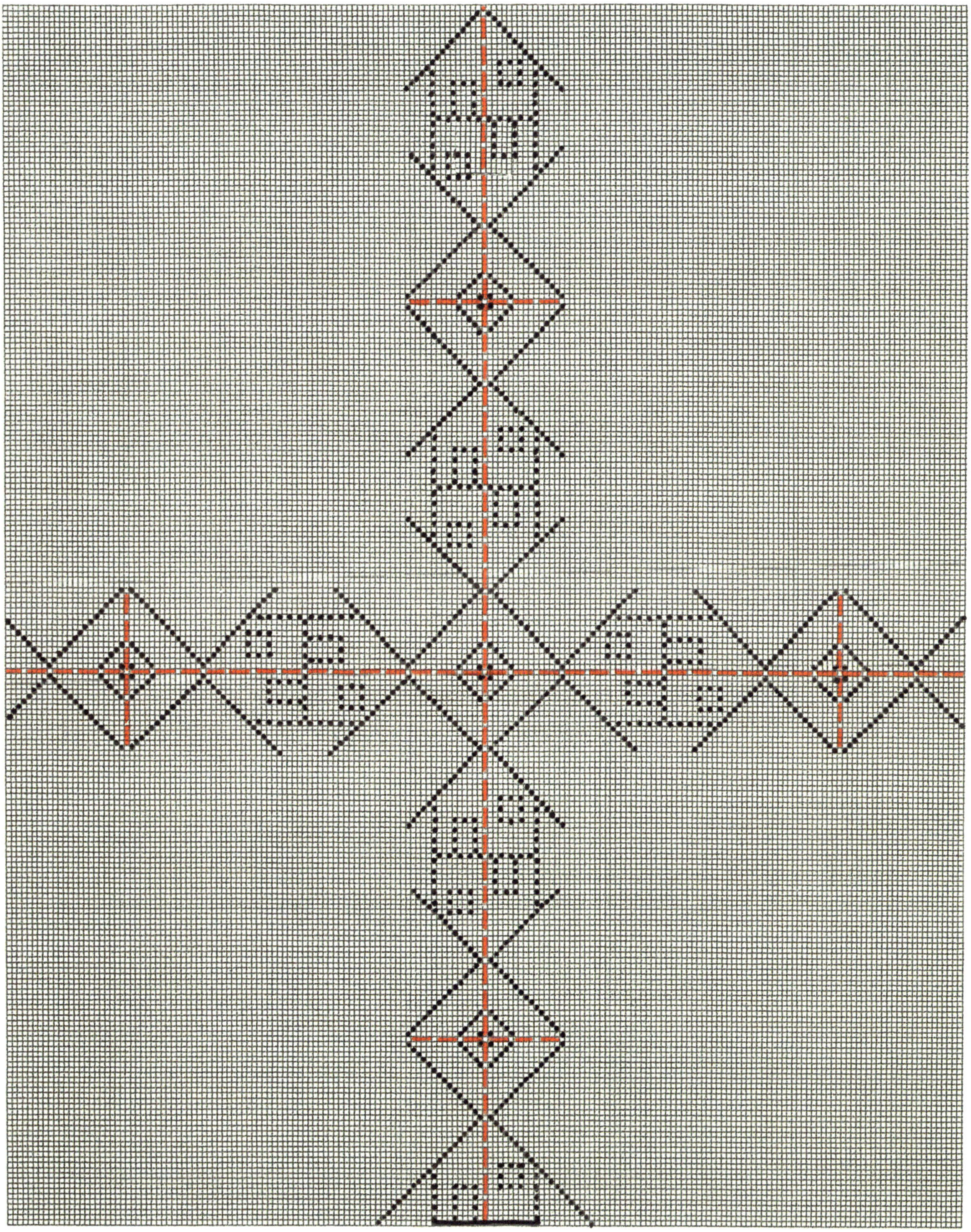

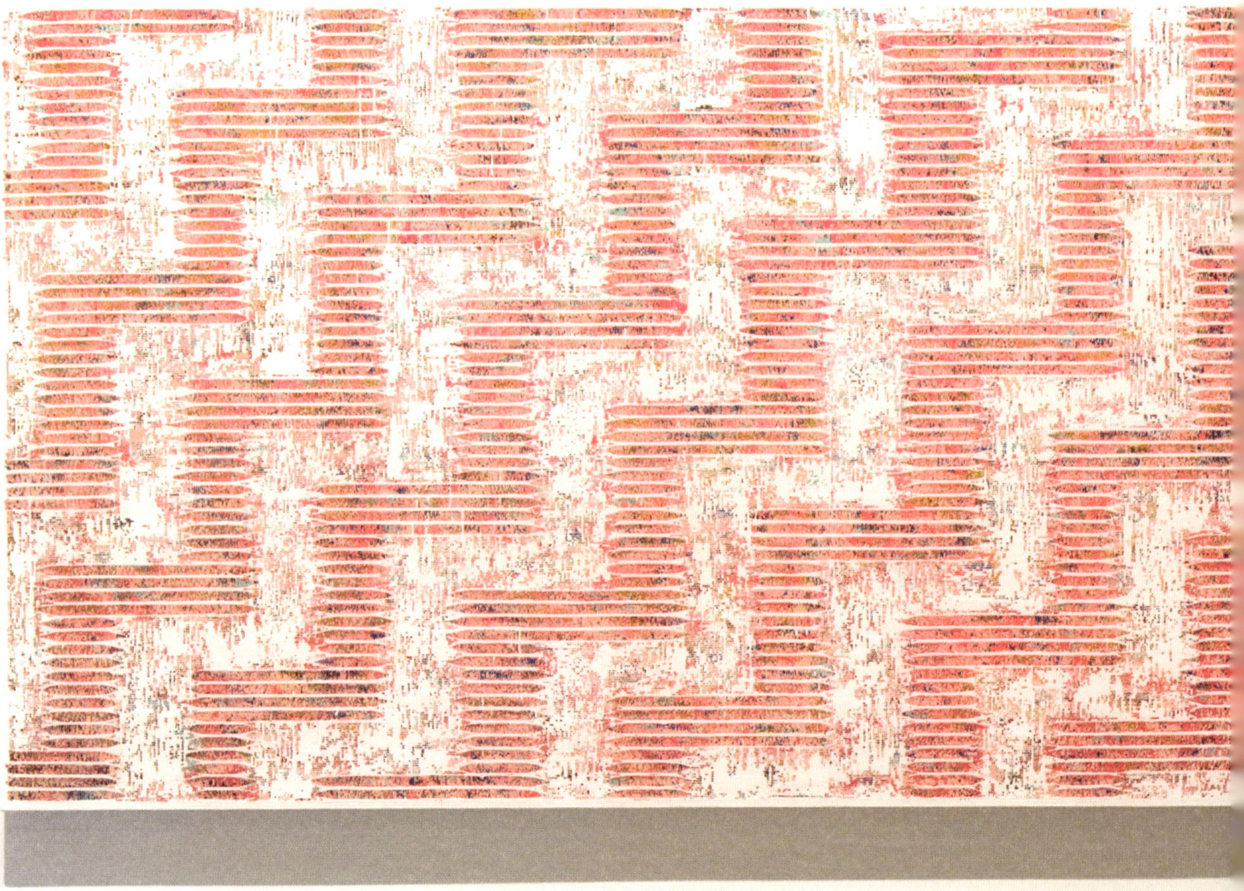

In other places you have been you recognise its absence, contrasting *there* with *here*. This hold on you is strange, because you have been *away* from this place for longer than you lived here. Ahead are the mountains and lake. You used to think of them as yours — and they are — but this inadequately describes your relationship. These mountains knew you for generations before you arrived — they have watched your line grow. You are equally *theirs* — they lay claim to you as much as you lay claim to them.

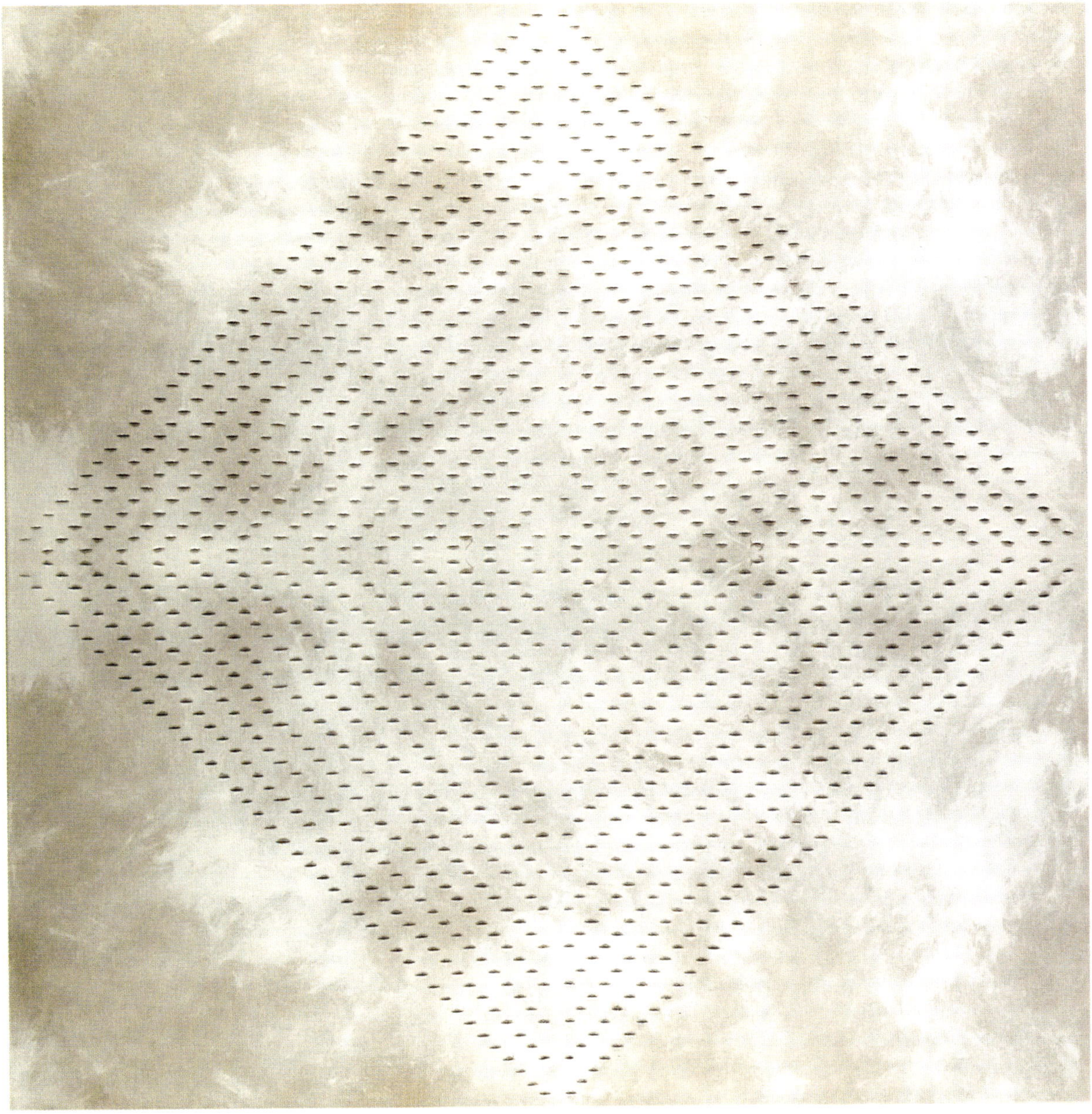

It might seem strange to go back to find a way forward — that sometimes retracing your steps is the best way to find your feet, to discover the path again. Why does your journey loop back around on itself so often? It seems like other people travel so easily in one direction, but you have always been drawn to the distractions along the way — a stop to take in the view, a seldom-visited place that seems interesting. When you were young, everyone you knew wanted to go abroad to see history, blind to murmurs here. The past in those places was allowed to shout. They had that same feeling of absence — for places their line had left behind generations ago. You left too, of course, but you did not find yourself there as they seemed to. If anything, you were a little lost.

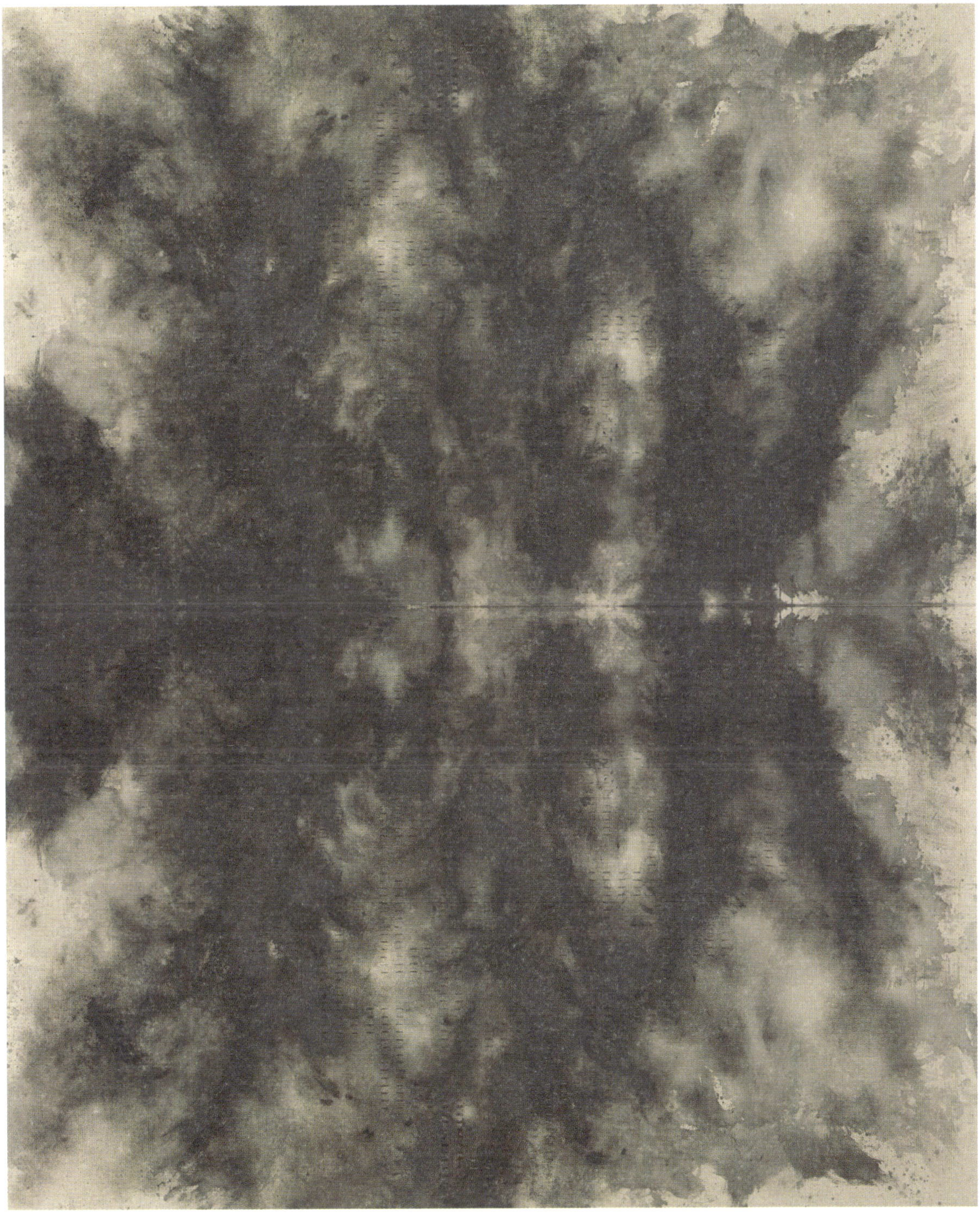

But here you are again, in the place you recognise. It is clear and calm on the lake. You look for any signs that the weather may change — a shift in light on the water, a darkness that could be a squall. You learnt to read this when you were young, you learnt the language of cloud and wind. You can trace your tūpuna in the contours of the bays — their names and stories are here. *You* are here. Share your breath with your mountain. Close your eyes and breathe through your nose, letting your nostrils flare. You are sharing the air, now warmed by your body, with this place.

Breathe in.

Breathe out.

Take a moment here. Acknowledge the space you occupy, the space you inhabit, the place you have returned to. Breathe in, letting the air expand your diaphragm and your lungs, breathe out, and your body contracts — your diaphragm curling back up into itself. Why haven't you recognised yourself in this shape before? Expansion and contraction: to spiral out, you must spiral in. You recognise the shape of this; it is told and retold in the pikopiko in the ground, in the eddies in the water, in the galaxies in the skies. You traced you fingers around takarangi carved in wood, traced your mind around it in pūrākau: in the contraction of Te Kore and the expanse of Te Pō.

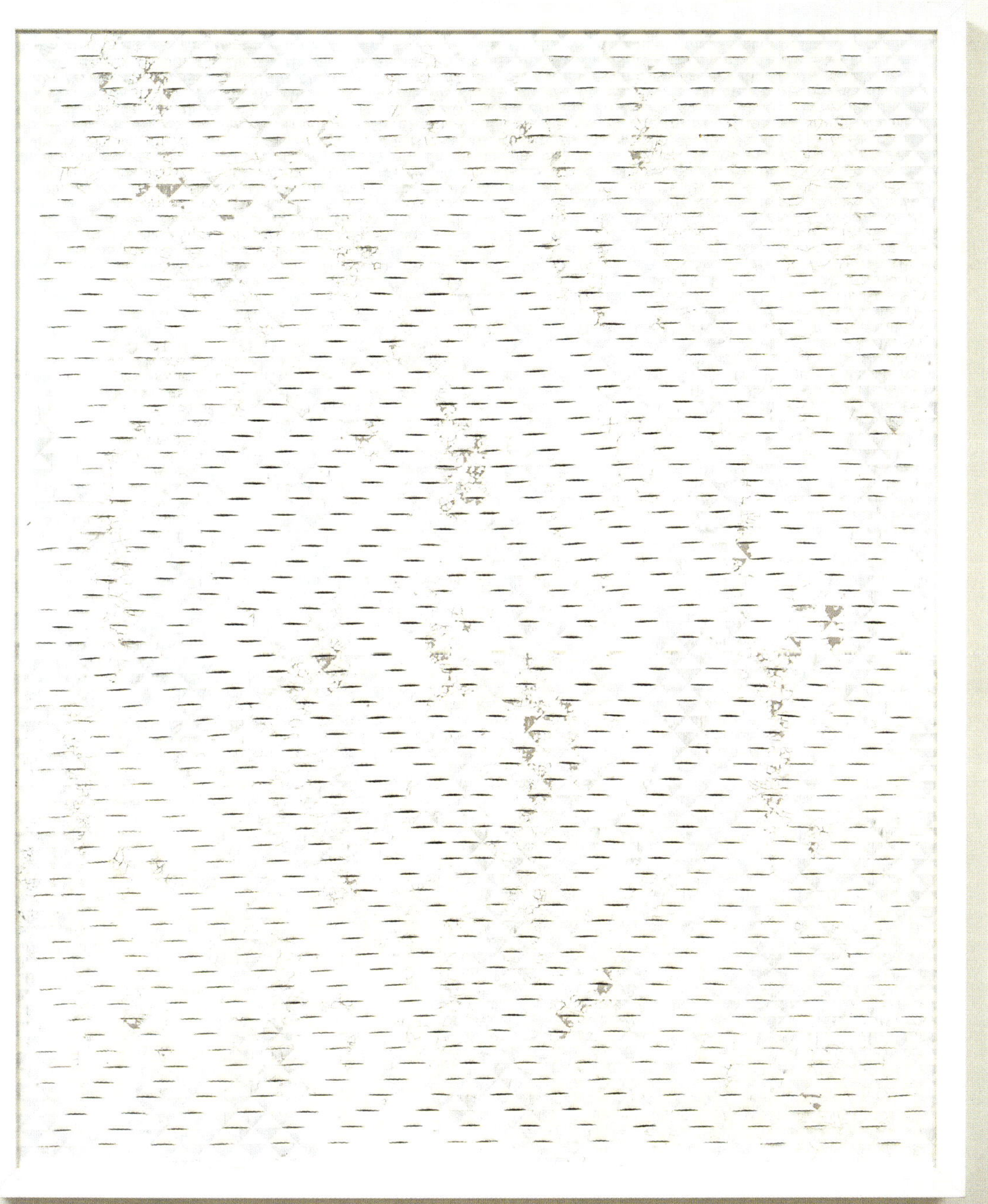

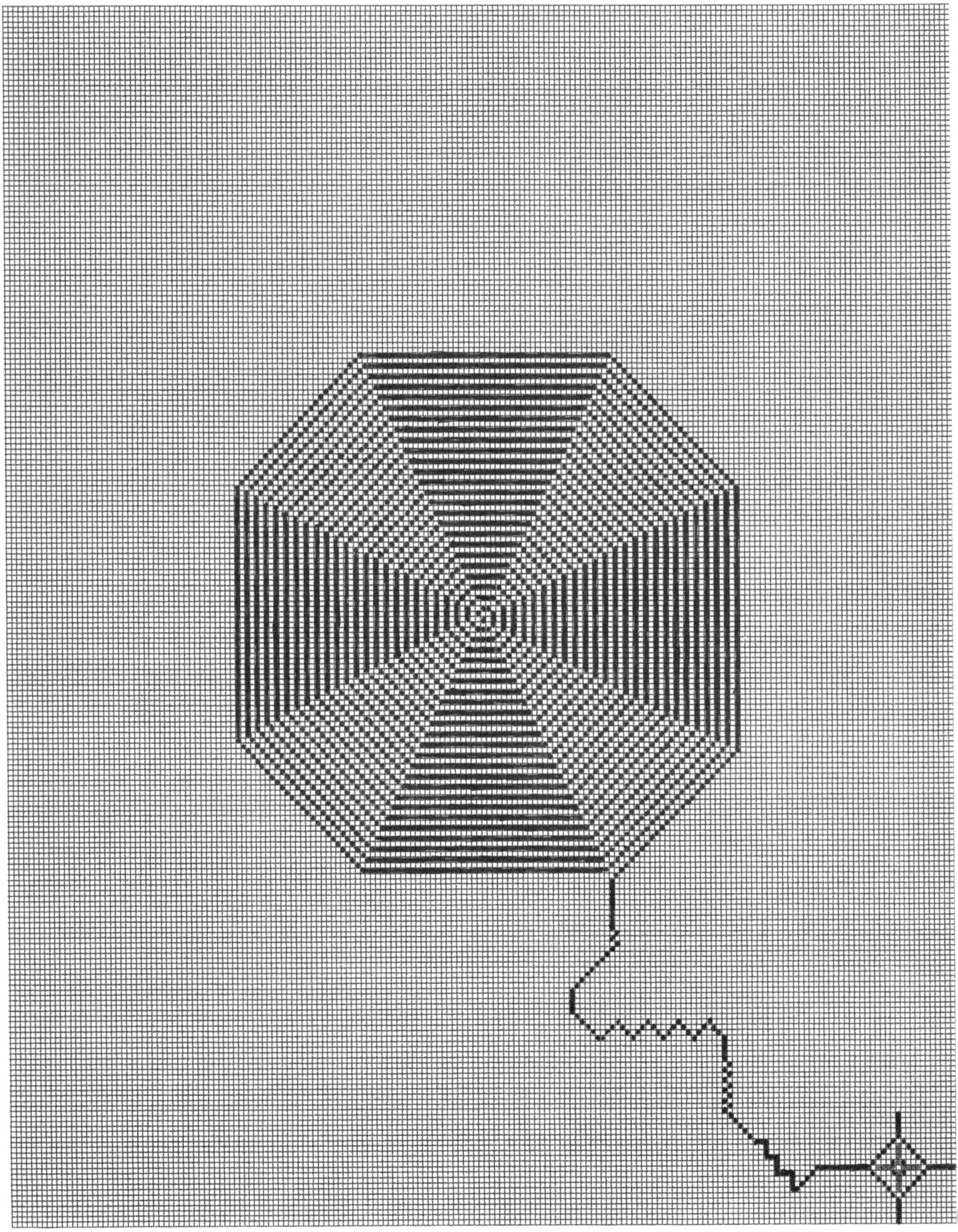

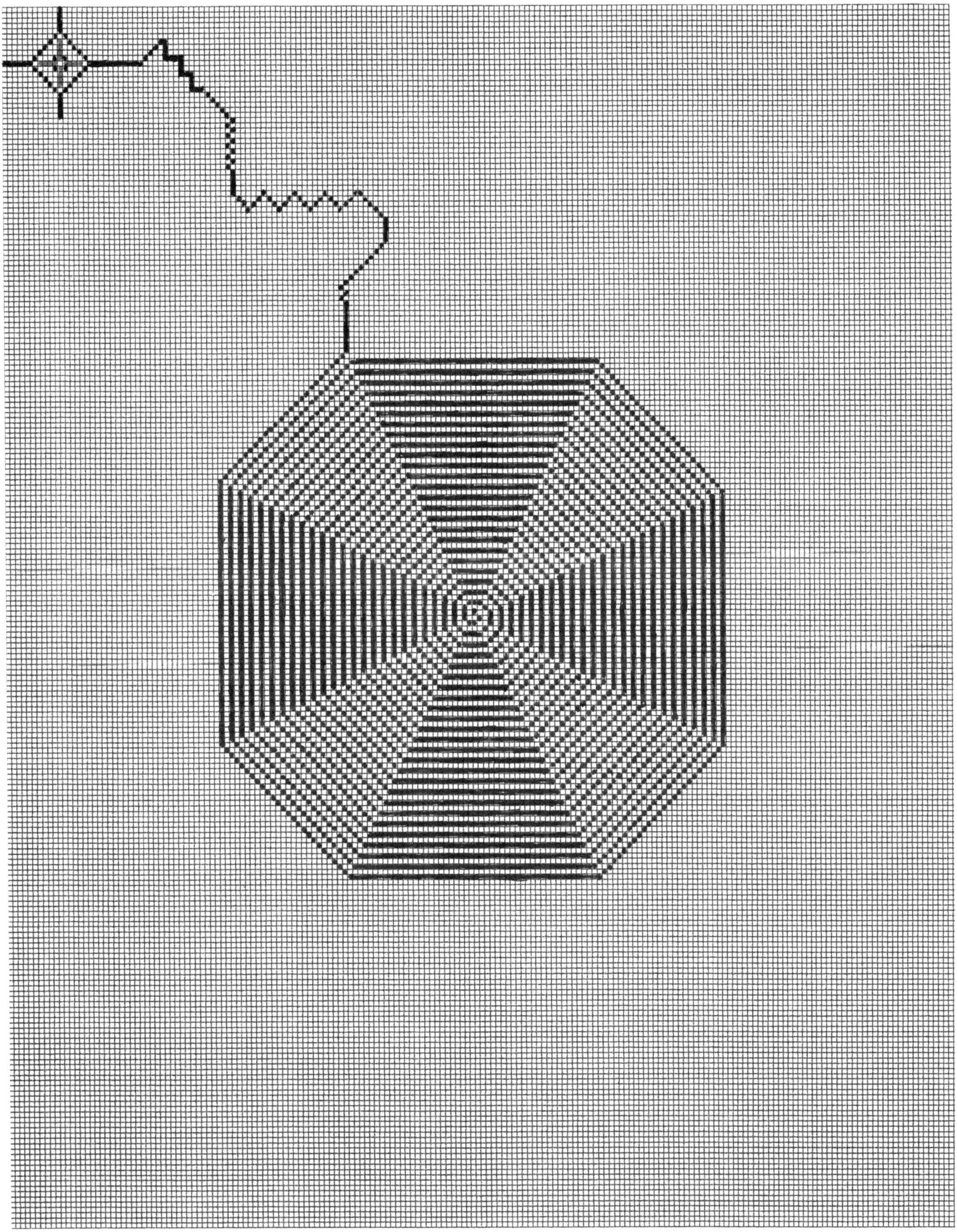

Your dad used to say you had bones here, and at the time you thought he was being literal — and he was, but he also was not. Yes, there are people who you have loved buried here, people who had loved you even though you did not exist when they were alive. Your bones *are* here, and *here* is in your bones. Here is in your people as much as your people are here.

And this shape is familiar too — te takarangi pulled out into a double helix: the threads and patterns of life. You are a culmination of them all. You carry the weight of all their decisions. This used to feel oppressive, like you didn't have any control of your life. Like your life wasn't yours alone. It is small enough here that everyone is woven together; the pattern of your life here seemed to be too rigid. And you didn't want that — you wanted a life free of ties, the freedom of anonymity, a story that was yours alone. But as you coloured your life, year by year and square by square, you saw them in your decisions and actions.

You thought of how lonely a self-made life would be — if there ever can be such a thing. There is no story that exists by itself; a story in its nature is about creating connections — moments in which we can see ourselves as we really are. Moments that join the past to the future, moments that join us together. You realised that you are a thread and a pattern: one of the strands of your whakapapa, twisting with all the others to make you whole.

Look at the motif in the tāniko, the harmony in the design: waharua kōpito, two diamonds, sitting end to end, stretching upwards — their points where people or events come together and expand. The shapes are like two mouths in conversation. Or does the shape remind you of your pito, your first scar after birth, a reminder of the cord that once supported you? They say that if you were wounded in combat, let it be here so everyone would know you were brave and faced your battle. Isn't your pito, then, a sign that you fought to be here?

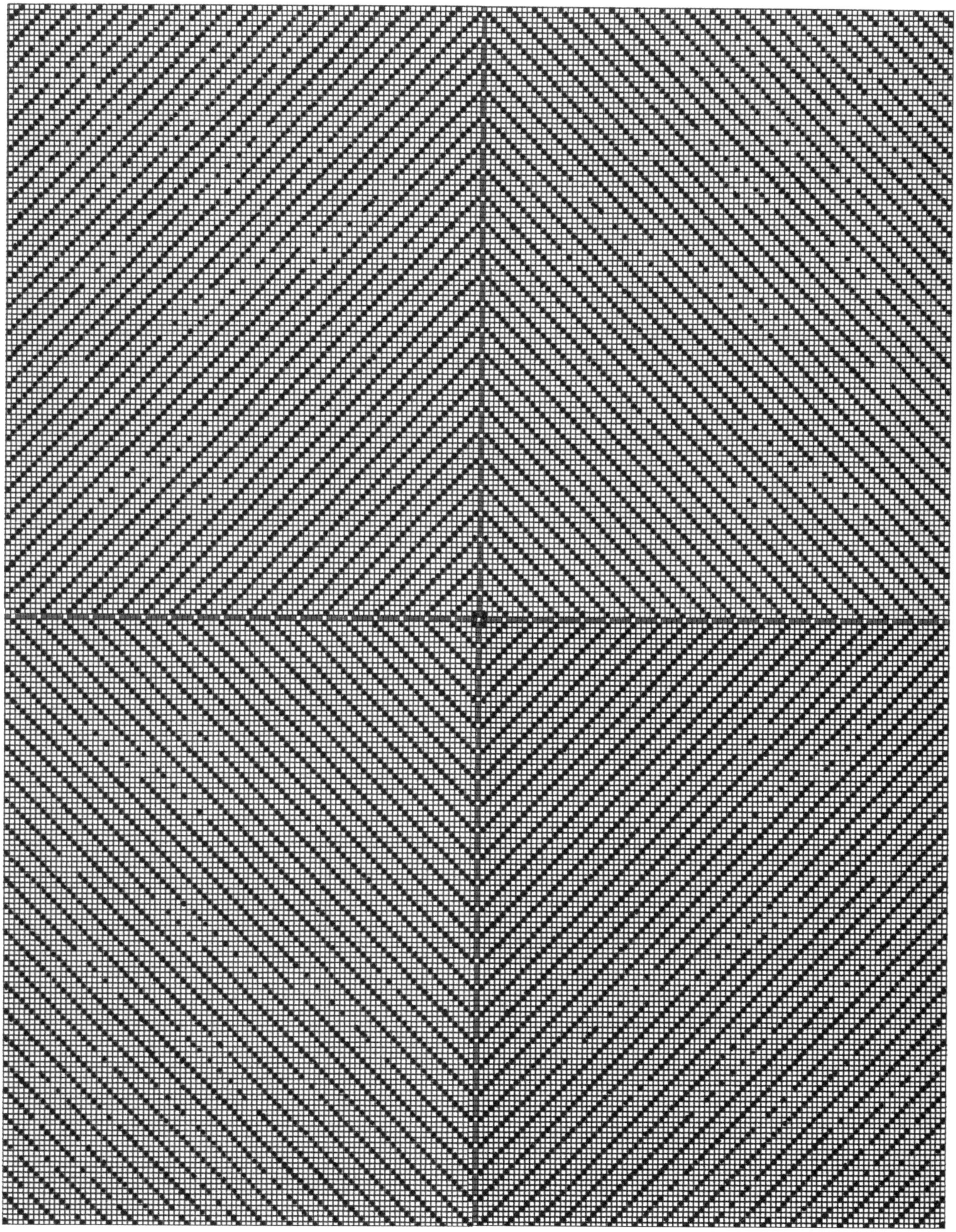

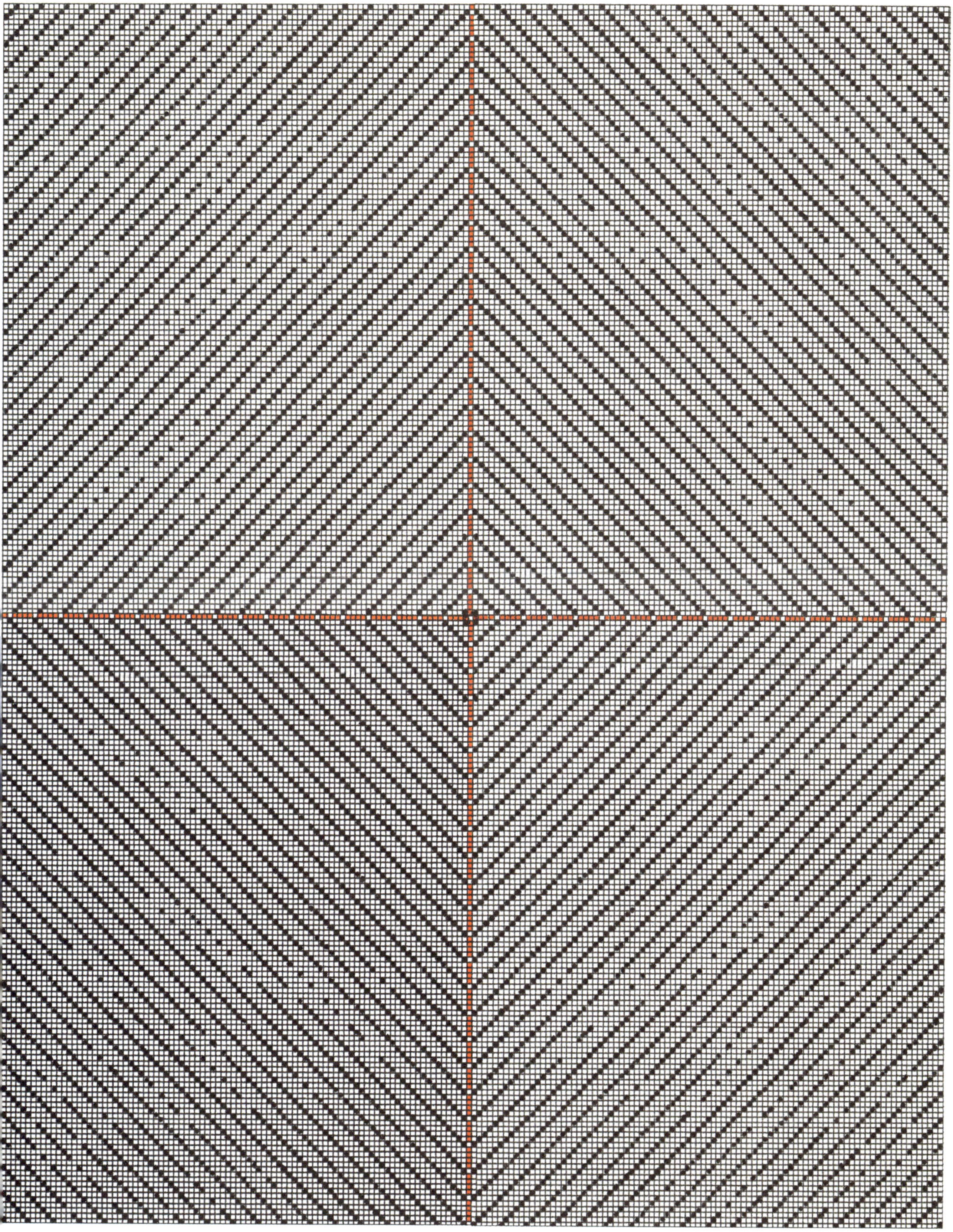

Are you here? Or have you spiralled in on yourself, the weight of your thoughts pulling you inwards?

Breathe in.

Breathe out.

You sit down on the shore and untie your shoelaces, easing off each shoe. You strip off your socks and tuck them into your shoes — useless tongues in a mouth that can't speak. The chill in the air bites at your toes, a hint of the frigid water ahead of you.

When you were at school you learnt that the lake stays at a steady temperature all year round. Snow-fed and so deep in some parts that the sun barely warms it. Even in the height of summer the water stayed ice-cream-headache cold. You'd dive in and it felt like the idea of you contracted — you became sharp and tight, tuna weaving among the lake weed. You would swim until your lips turned blue and until you couldn't control your shivers anymore. You'd swim to the raft to bake in the sun, the wood soaked and slimy from other wet bodies. Once warm, you'd dive in again — there was not enough height for any cool manus, but sometimes you would get a decent bomb and shower everyone else on the raft with your triumph. You shudder with the memory of your belly flops, skin stinged pink, but the worst sting was the laughter that you could hear under the water before you surfaced. In those times you wished that you could swim down, down, down to the darkest, deepest point and never resurface again. But then your lungs would scream for air, and you'd swim up and break the film between you and your humiliation. You'd play it off like you meant to do it, even as your red skin betrayed your lies.

You used to swim here no matter the weather, sun, rain, cold; it didn't even matter to you. The world is changeable, but the water stays the same. You've lost that sense of imperviousness somewhere through the years.

Today it is too cold to swim, but you will paddle in the water. The stones on the shore shift beneath your weight. They are cold underfoot, but you have the memory of them in summer, smooth but so hot you would hop like you had stood on a prickle. Why is the past always summer and the future always winter?

The water is painfully cold; you repeat the words *a steady 12 degrees* like the mantra will make the temperature bearable. You keep your feet on top of the lakebed a while, wanting to stay present in the moment. Your toes go numb, but it feels like the rest of you is waking. Now you can't stand the cold any longer, and you sway your hips, digging your feet down, down, down, and they are warmed by the rock beneath — the relatively thin layer between you and the lava of this active caldera. *A steady 12 degrees* because the massive body of water is heated by the massive crater it is in.

The landscape here was created by earthquake and eruption — sudden shifts in being. When you left here you thought that you too could be suddenly changed, forged in disruption: a new place, a new style, a new you. You have always been attracted to the overt display: roman candles over sparklers.

Instead, your change is like the stones on the shore — a process of erosion and sediment. It is by persistence, not sudden upheaval. The nerves in your feet crackle with the warmth, and it is the good sort of pain that reminds you that you're alive. That you are here.

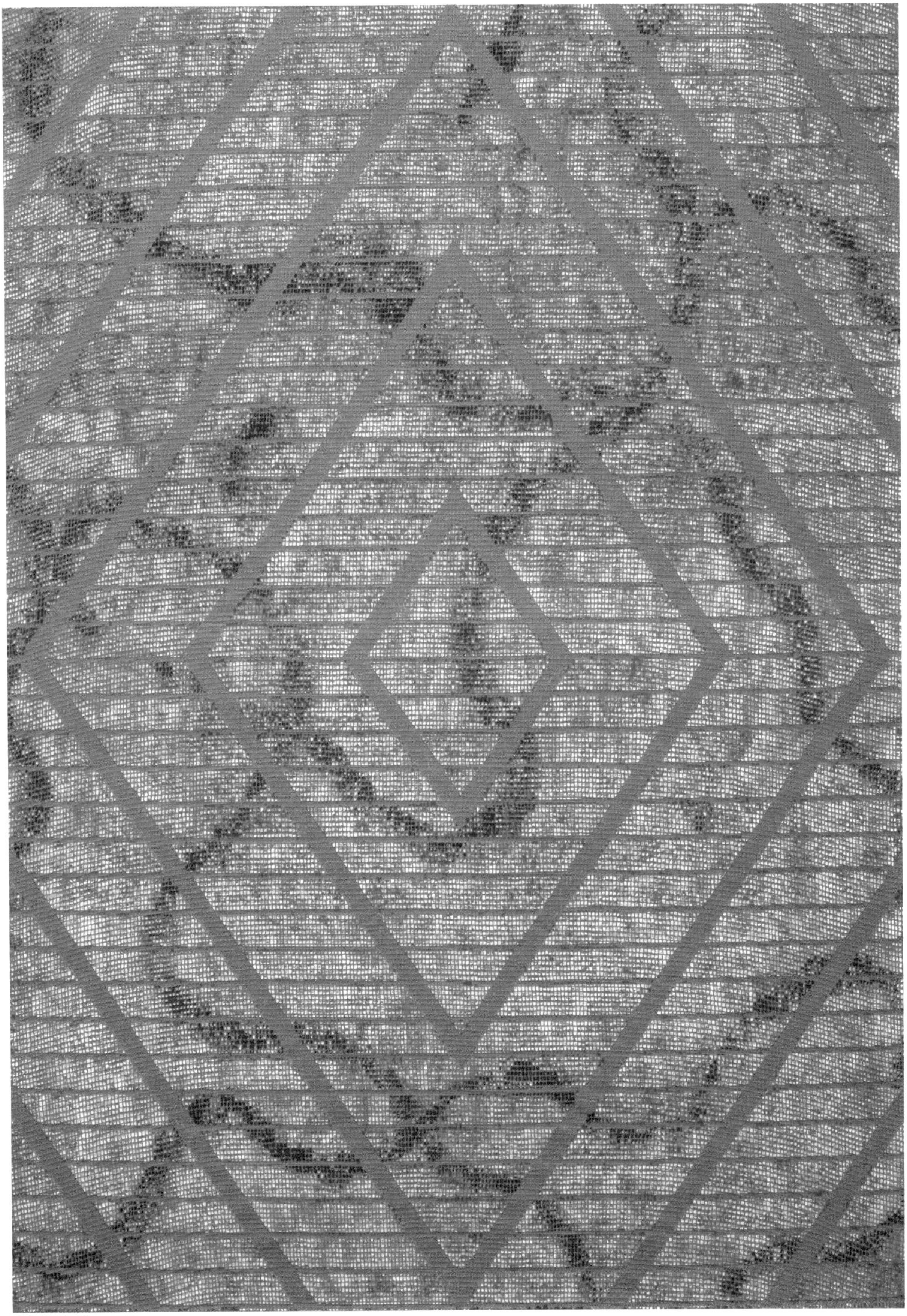

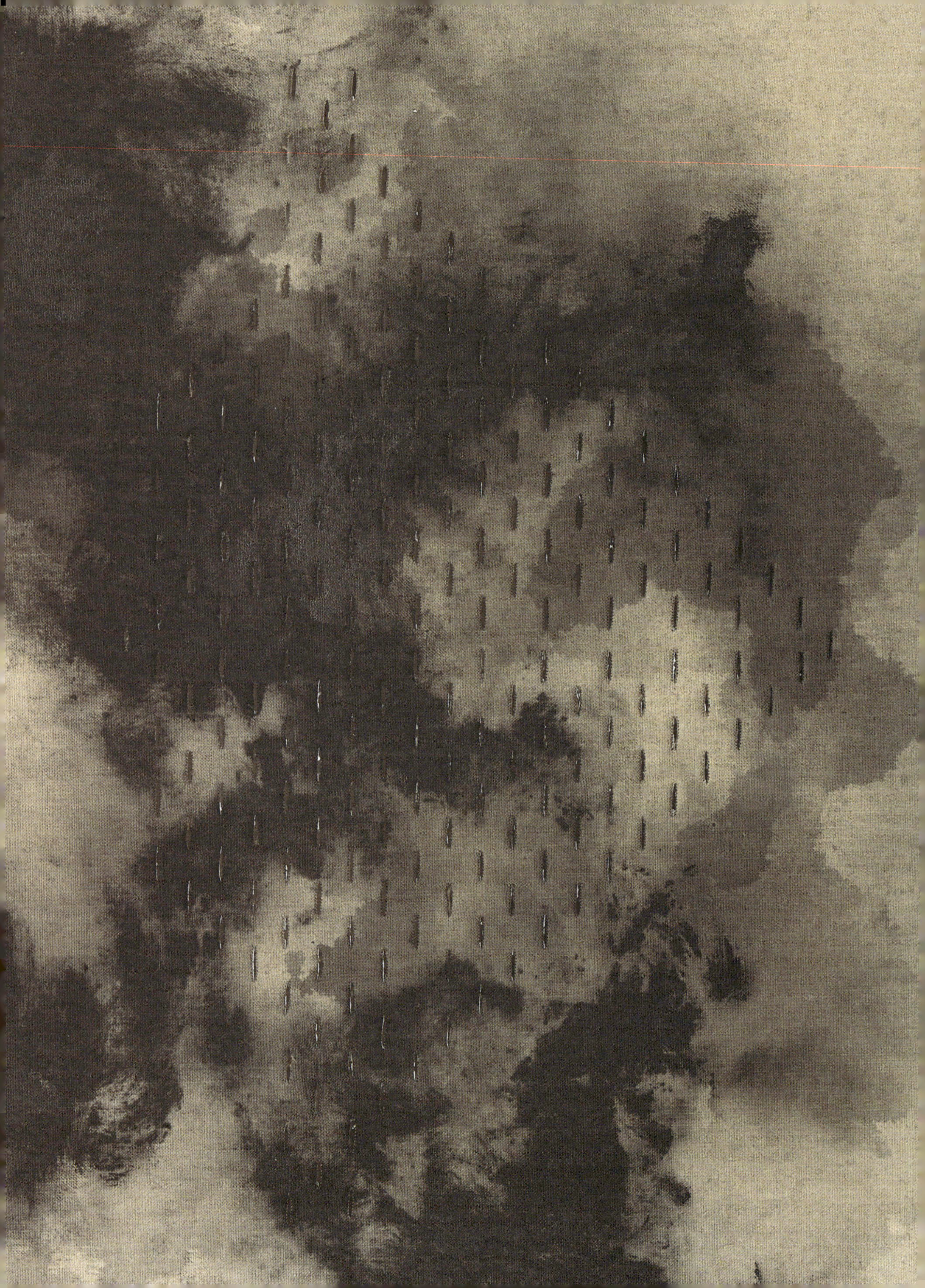

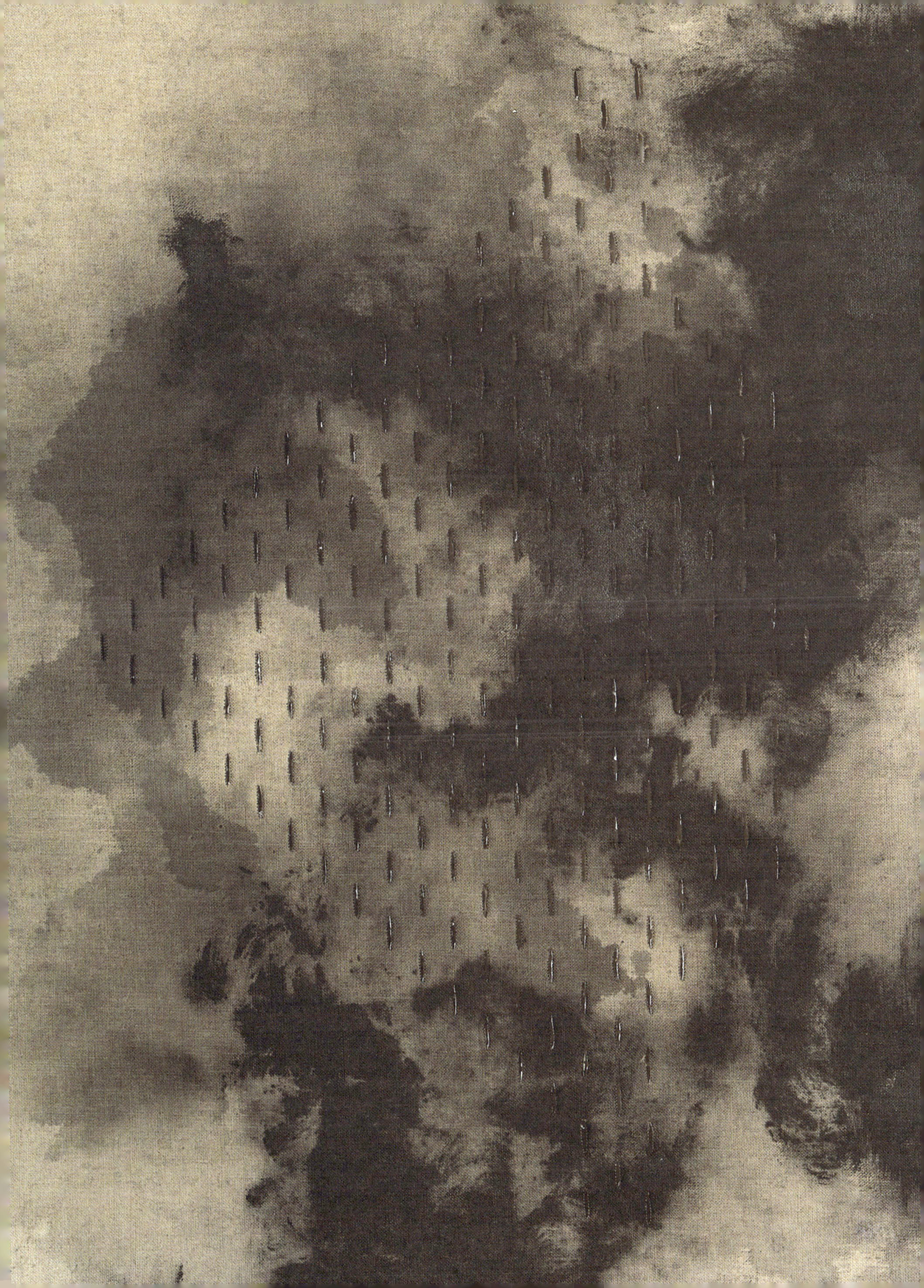

You can't stay here forever. You lift your feet from the lakebed and walk back feeling the resistance of the water. Of yourself. The stones on shore shift beneath your feet and you pretend that it is just them that slow you. You use your socks to brush the little bit of sand that still clings to your feet. Toes still wet shoved into socks and shoes, skin rubbed red with every step. You're not in pain; your chafed skin is an annoyance — yes — but not painful. But your mind goes back to a fairy tale from far away and long ago. A mermaid steps on her newly made feet and it feels as if she treads upon knives and needles: that is the price you pay for rejecting yourself. And it saddens you that this is the story you think of, that it is so readily in your mind, and yet your own pūrākau are missing. It is sort of grimly funny that the story that you think about, a story about losing your voice, losing your identity, is one that was imposed upon you. If you were feeling generous, then you might think that was because some stories are universal, but today it just proves how deeply disconnected you have become from yourself. Although you didn't have the choice like that mermaid: your tongue was *taken*, not given.

You know you have work to do, and it seems like there is not enough time to do it all. How long does it take to free your tongue from the straps and statutes that first bound it? From the shame and sorrow that keeps it still? The mamae you feel isn't yours alone — it is a hurt that reverberates across and through your people. And you are not so far removed from the wound; it happened only a couple of lifetimes ago. Within your grandparents' lifetime you were considered part of a dying race, so to kill your language was thought a sort of kindness, an enlightenment, although without reason. Within your parents' lifetime children were still punished for speaking by an education system that spent so much energy lessening knowledge. Within your lifetime people proudly pronounce *croissant* and *brie* but refuse to learn how to say the name of the town they grew up in, preferring to strangle the vowels in their mouth while claiming it is not ignorance. You should take them at their word — not ignorance, no. Their hate is absolutely deliberate.

You must be deliberate too. Don't hold your tongue for their comfort anymore: they have never considered yours.

Consider this, then: if so much can be destroyed in a few short lifetimes, what could be achieved in the next few? You look at the next generation and marvel at how much they know already. You hope that some of the mamae ends with you.

The map of your mind can be redrawn; there is no need to keep to the narrows of an old-world view. You can be expansive. You can make new pathways; you can broaden the ones you already have. You can delight in the kupu shaping your mouth, the physicality of language: tongue and teeth and breath and throat. You hope that one day you will connect it all: sight, sound, meaning.

Ah, but that bright, sharp sting hobbles you again. The anger that you have to do this, the work of reclaiming yourself. Sometimes it overwhelms you and you get lost in the rage of it — what more could you do in life if you didn't need to spend this time fighting for something that just should have been yours? You remember a conversation from a decade or two ago, when learning seemed futile because even if you could speak, who would you speak *to*? You smart at the memory of your younger self, because even though you were isolated from your community — partly by your own doing — it was really because you were scared. Of failure. Of not being enough. Of not belonging.

It has taken you a long time to realise that this is part of your journey too — that there are old scripts to unlearn. That for you it is not as simple as memorising kupu and phrases and syntax — it is carving yourself true: reshaping, or perhaps restoring, your outline.

For a long time, you've thought of it as your cross to bear, but perhaps you've been carrying a pou — and no one expects you to carry this on your own. That is your old way of thinking — that you are alone. There are many people who will carry it with you.

Travel north of town and inland to your marae. You've never visited as an adult, so your only memories are from when you were a child: fizzy drink at a hākari, long speeches that you didn't understand.

You feel a bit uncomfortable, because in some ways you are a stranger here: you have been away for a very long time. This is the place that you tell people you are from: after maunga, after moana, after iwi — you are here, but have you ever been present?

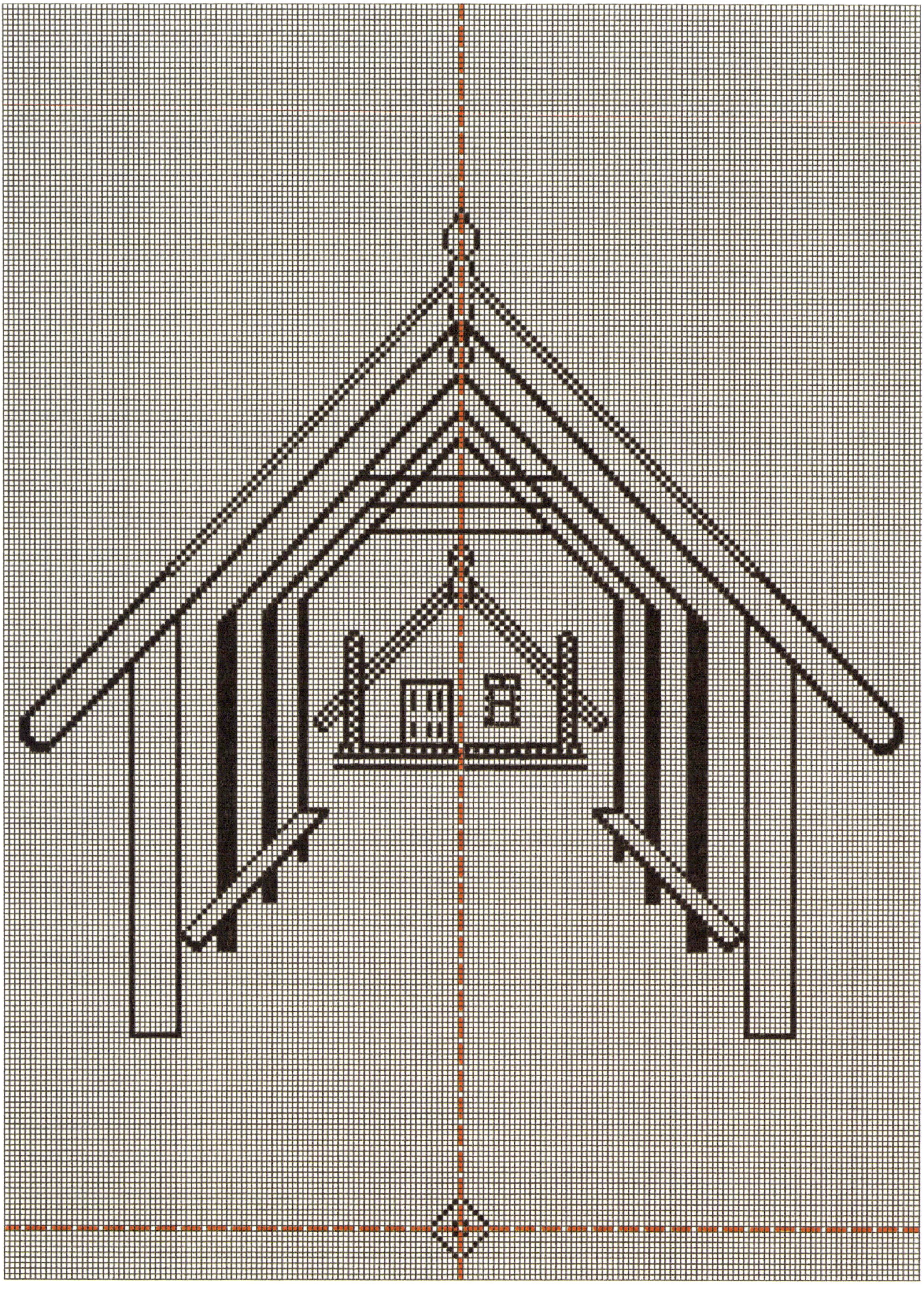

You take your shoes off once more to enter the wharenui. It is a relief to be free of them again. You step inside, almost tip-toeing, unsure if this place will accept the measure of you. On the back wall there are framed portraits. You recognise some of the people, aunts, uncles, cousins you had met a long time ago.

Some of these people you know only through photos, but in them you see a map to yourself. The slight asymmetry of your eyes present three generations ago, the shape of your face in a cousin who found you online. You know them only from stories, but in them you see a story of yourself.

You breathe in and out. You *are* here.

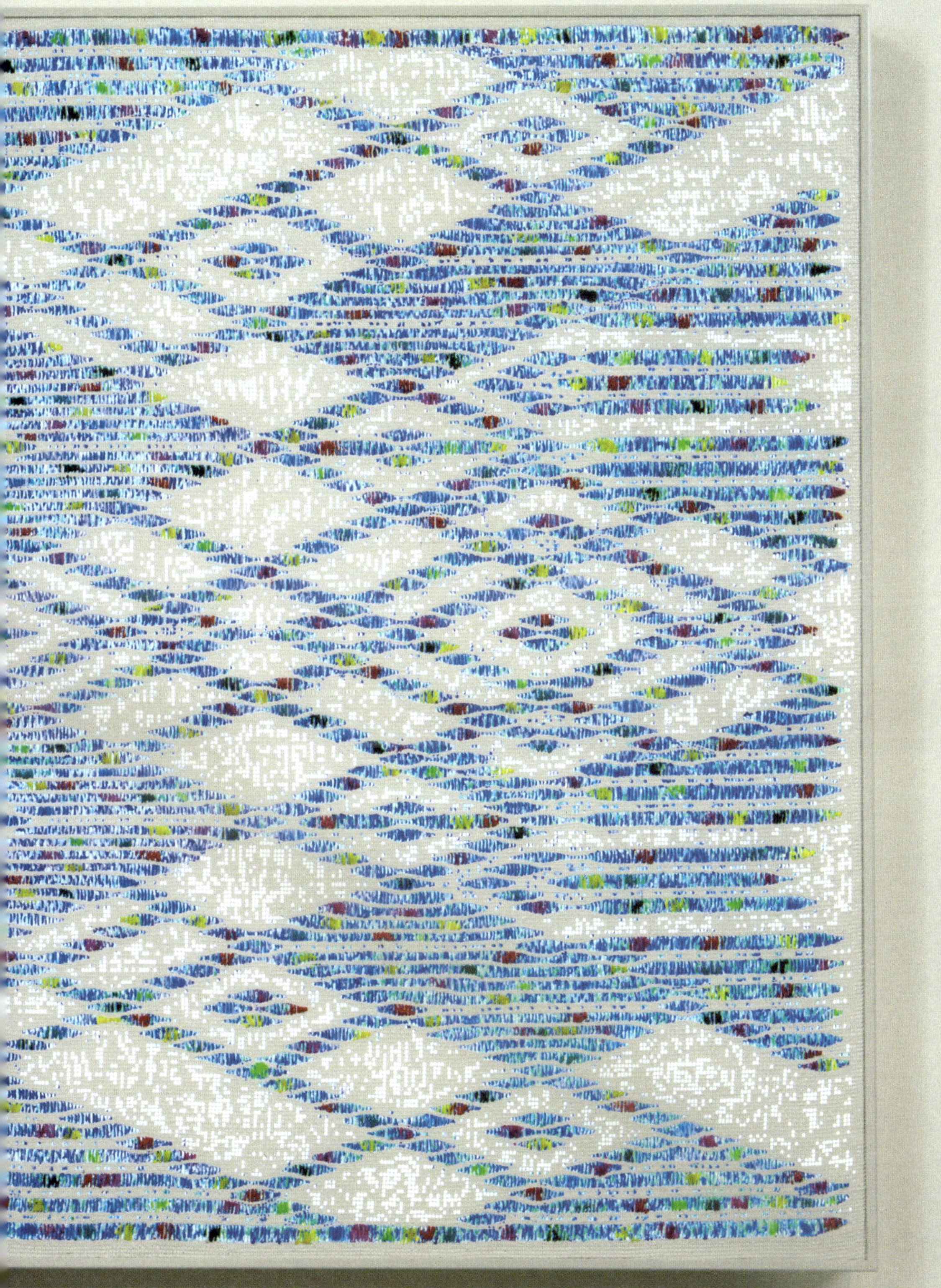

There is a certain kind of bravery that you think you lack. When you were a kid, the bravest of the brave would jump off Bulli Point. Your dad would take you all on the short, summertime drive from town to Motutere. The camping ground there was full of tourists, but the Point was mostly locals. Most of the jumpers would take a big run-up before they launched themselves into the sky, letting themselves drop down into the lake, down, down, down. Then they would clamber up the cliff face to do it again. Some would just walk off the ledge, nonchalant about the risk and seemingly uncaring about the admiration of those around them — but of course they *must* have cared, who wouldn't? They would just step into the air, trusting that gravity would be kind to them. Trusting themselves.

Was it admiration or envy that left you breathless as you watched them leap? Your skin burning in the summer sun, you yearned for that cold lake water. But there were no half-measures at the Point, no ledges that were not as high. No steps for babies. You had a choice when you looked down from the top of that cliff, down the couple of storeys to the water below: you jumped, or you didn't.

And you didn't.

You have been brave at other times in your life, of course. But there's something in your hesitation now that makes you feel like that kid afraid of that edge. Was it how far you would fall that scared you? Or the worry that once you knew the thrill of falling you would seek it out again and again? Or regret about all the time you wasted on the ground?

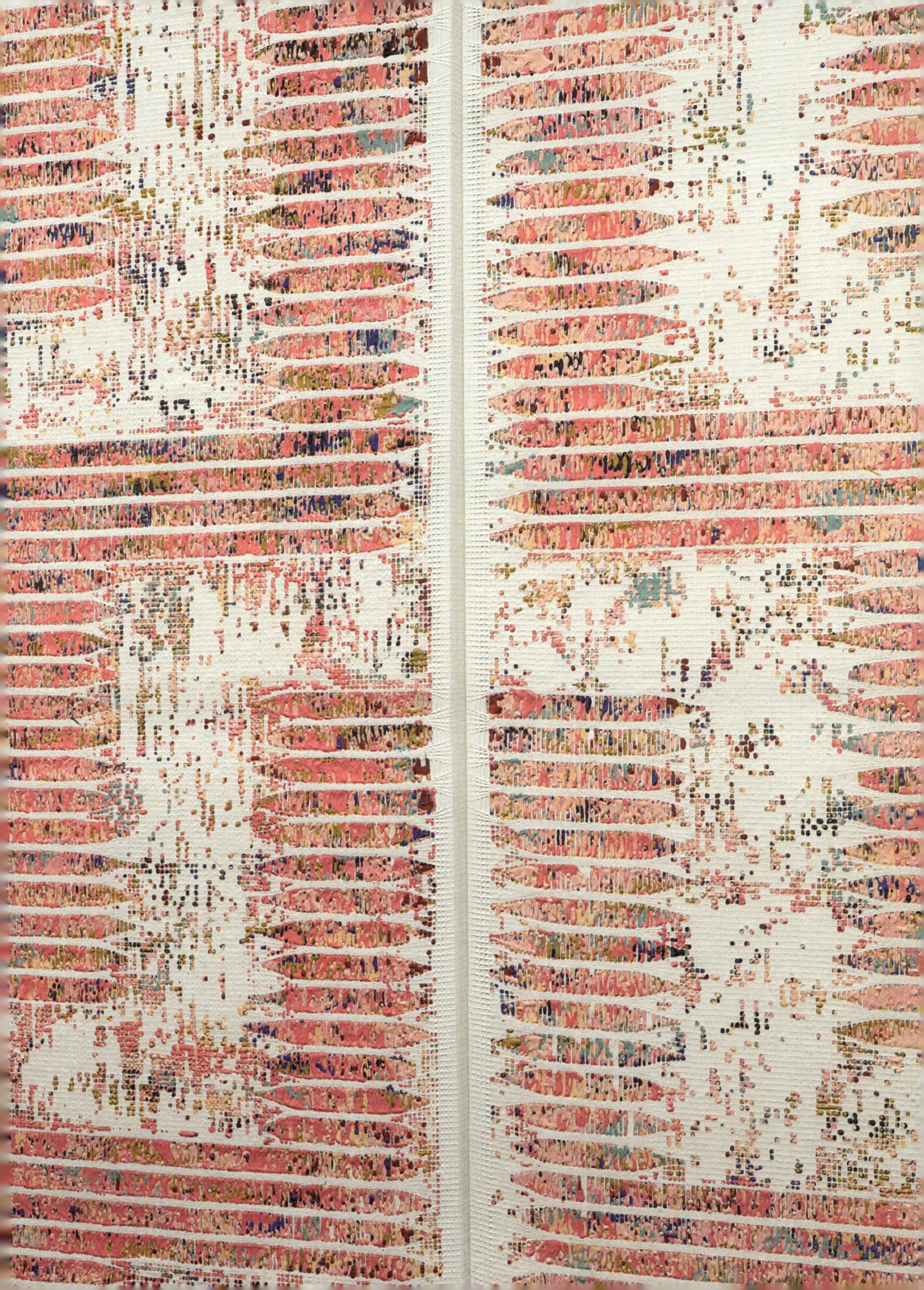

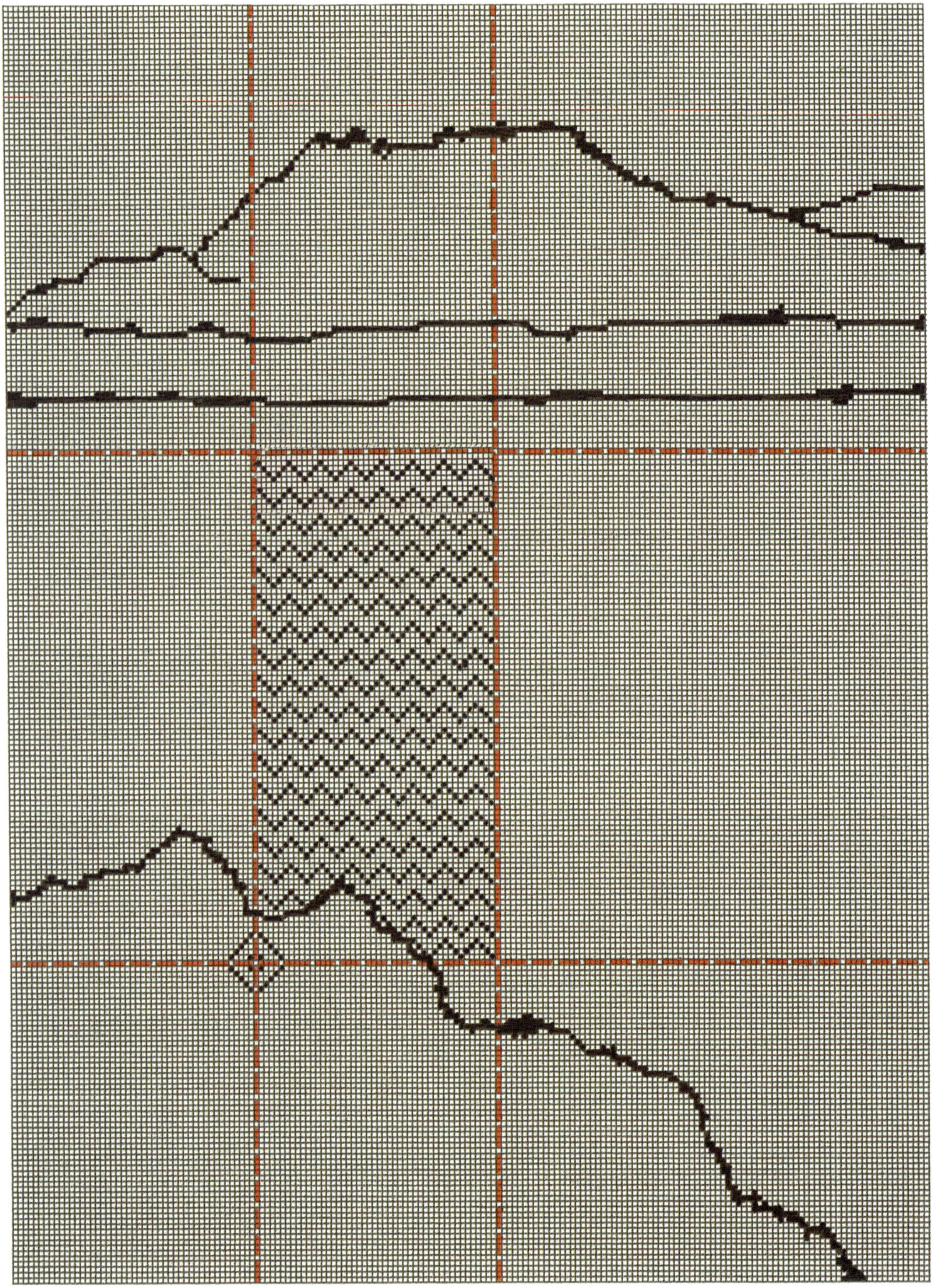

What is it that stops you now?

Is it the possibility of failure? You've survived failure many times before, so why would this be different? Perhaps you have tied too much to your ability to speak, to understand. Because it is more than understanding a language — it is making sense of yourself.

And perhaps there is nothing more frightening than reckoning with yourself.

If your life were a movie, you'd jump off the Point now, despite the cold and being fully clothed. You wouldn't even pause to take off your shoes: the camera would zoom in on them as you pushed yourself up and off, the camera following behind you off the edge. The footage would slow as you made your descent — perhaps a shot or two of you as a child would be cut in to make the point that you had grown into your bravery. And as you sank into the water, you would hang suspended there in the dappled shadows, at peace until your need to fill your lungs would tip your head up towards the light. And then it would cut to you surfacing again, laughing — that circle in your life completed at last. You faced your childhood fear and now you can face *anything*.

How disappointing it is then to still quake at the edge of the Point — perhaps more afraid now than as a child, even though you don't really have more to lose. Why do you think that because you've never jumped from here you lack courage? Why have you returned to this place at all?

You know that you are brave. That this is not the cliff you need to conquer. The seven-metre plunge from the rocks to the lake is not the leap you need to complete. You seek a different kind of immersion — not in the cool clear water below, but in the waters of your soul.

Breathe out.

Breathe in.

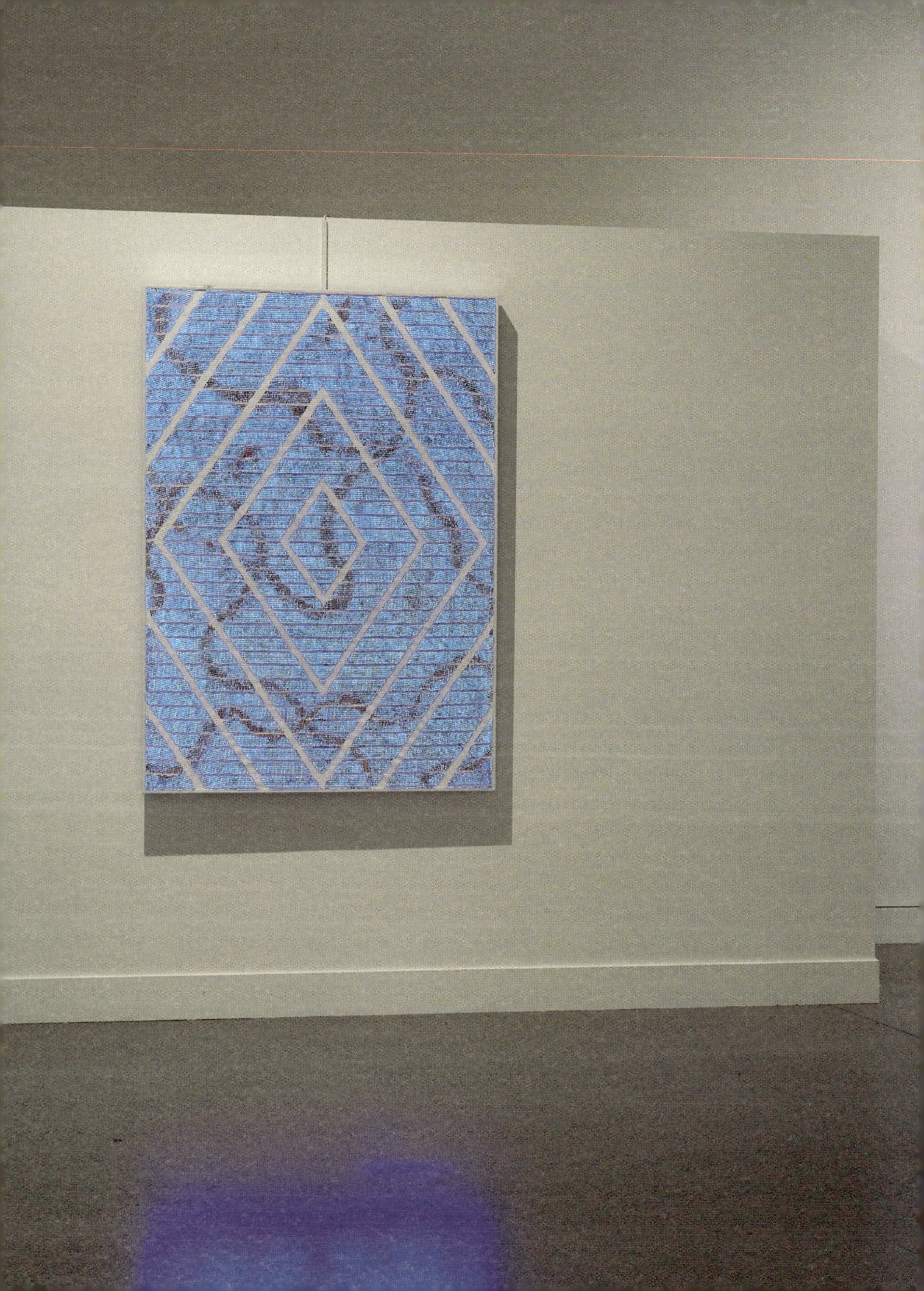

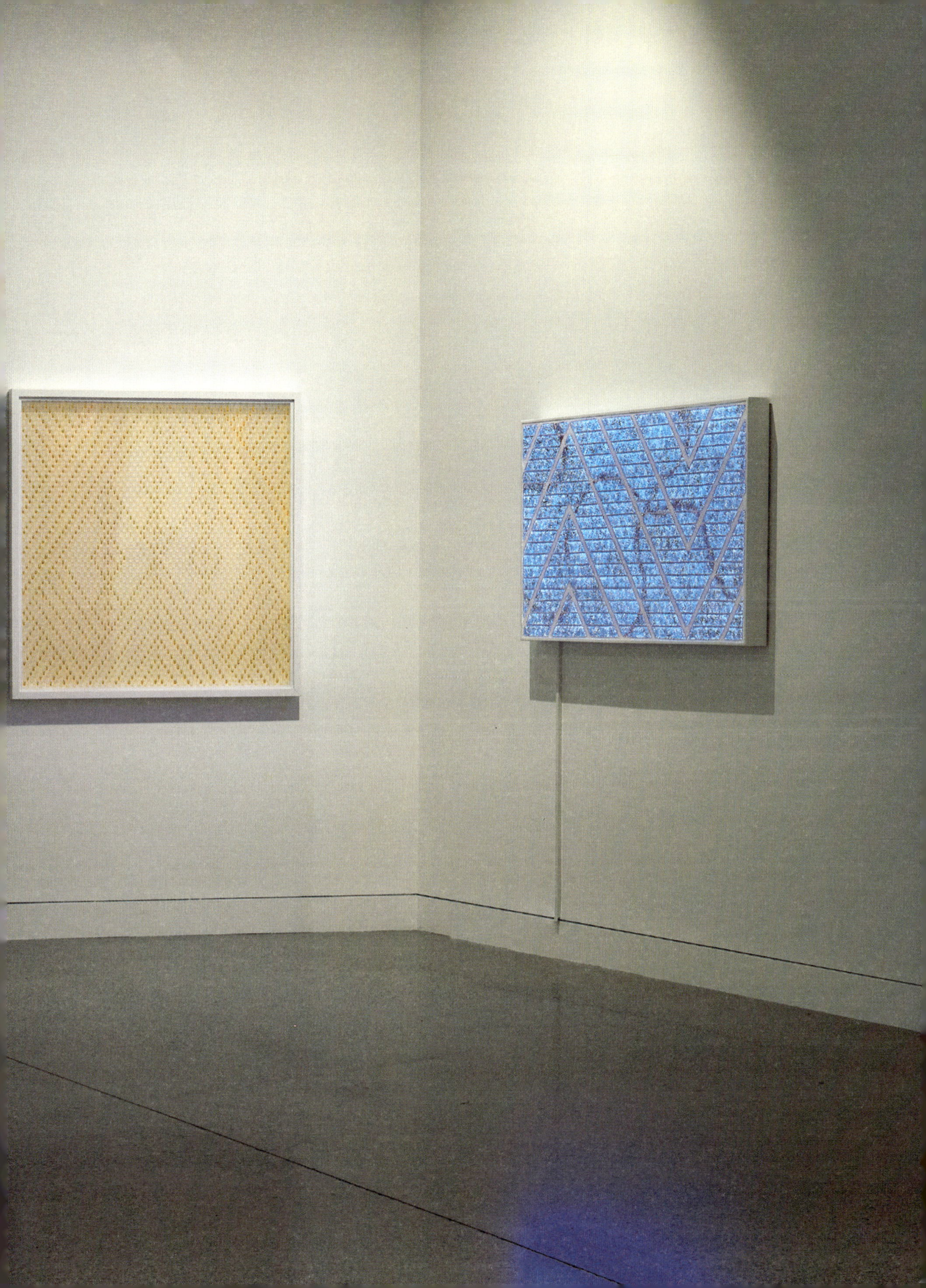

These new kupu are reclaiming space in your synapses. Did you need as many tools to create these paths as you do now to modify them? Examples, metaphors, stories, context. You try to remember if this is what it was like when you learnt your first language, when the pattern, shapes and sounds finally became clear and you understood. An example: you know mārama because you think of te marama — understanding is as clear and bright as the full moon.

Sometimes you lose track of words and kupu, mixing them up in your head and on your tongue. It is hard to break old habits — the mispronunciations you learnt as a child, the way you hold your mouth letterbox thin, so all your vowel sounds flatten into one. You dig the heel of your hand into the tight muscles at the base of your jaw to free the space for these more expansive vowels that round your palate.

To start with your r's sound more like d's until your tongue is strong enough to flick into a trill. Sometimes your mouth aches like you have been laughing and laughing — it is the pain of joy.

There are things that you've just learnt that excite you — connections between word and place and history. You had thought that Bulli Point was named after cockabullies — the small fish were plentiful in the water there. Or perhaps someone was feeling poetic and thought the jumpers swimming back to the cliff looked like a school of the fish.

Now you know it is a corruption of a kupu: perhaps Te Pōroro, the name of the marae that once stood here. Or perhaps of the poroporo that grows along the cliff edge. Even if it was named for cockabullies, that too is a corruption of kōkopu. You have a list of these words — biddybid, Otago, Tolaga — and some of the stories of how the kupu slid into the space between Māori and English. That space that strangely still exists *now*.

You decide that you will call this place by its name — it is the smallest courtesy, and you know how annoying it is when people get your name wrong, turning you into a star, or a number, or a week, pronouncing you *wrong*.

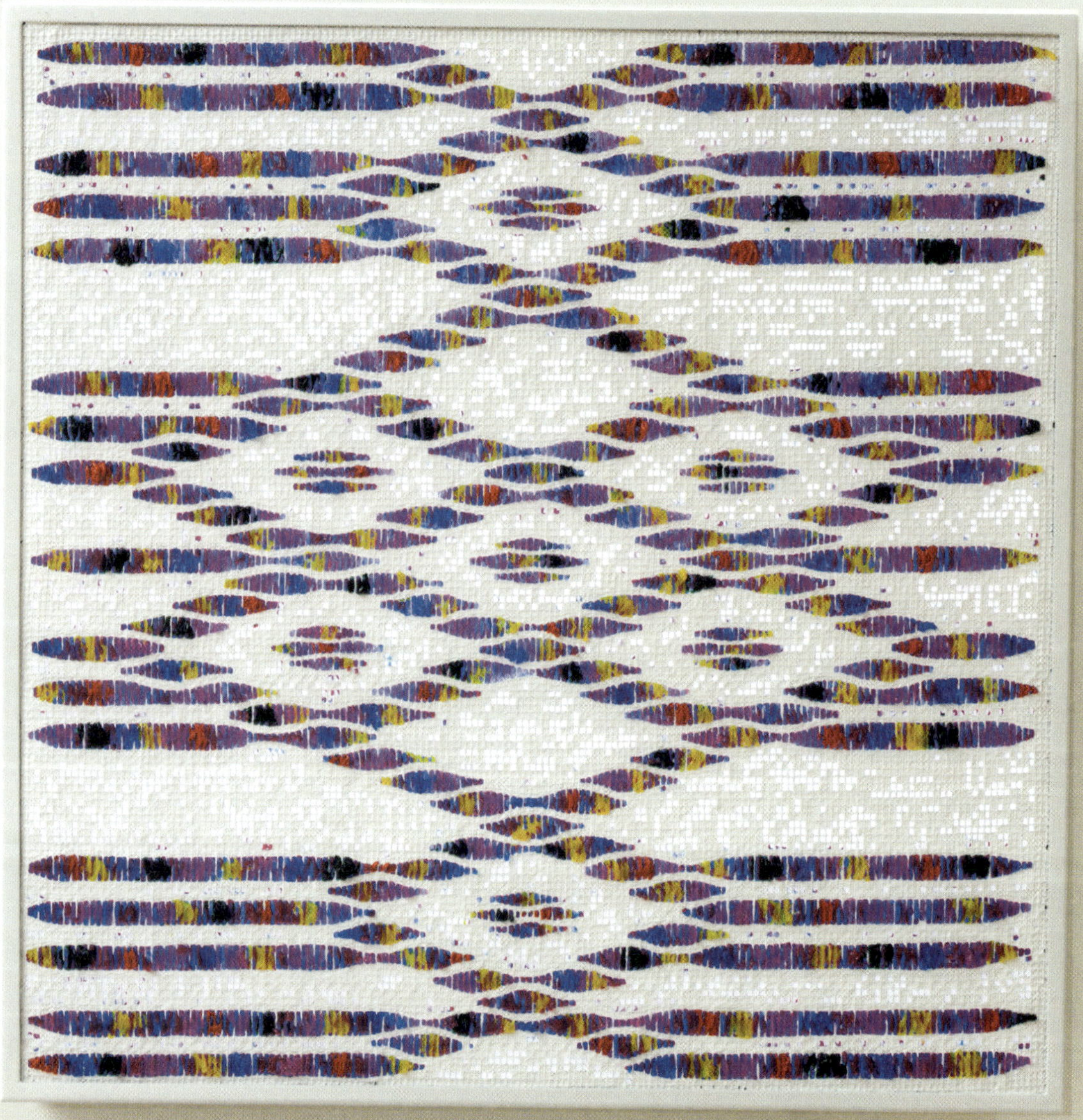

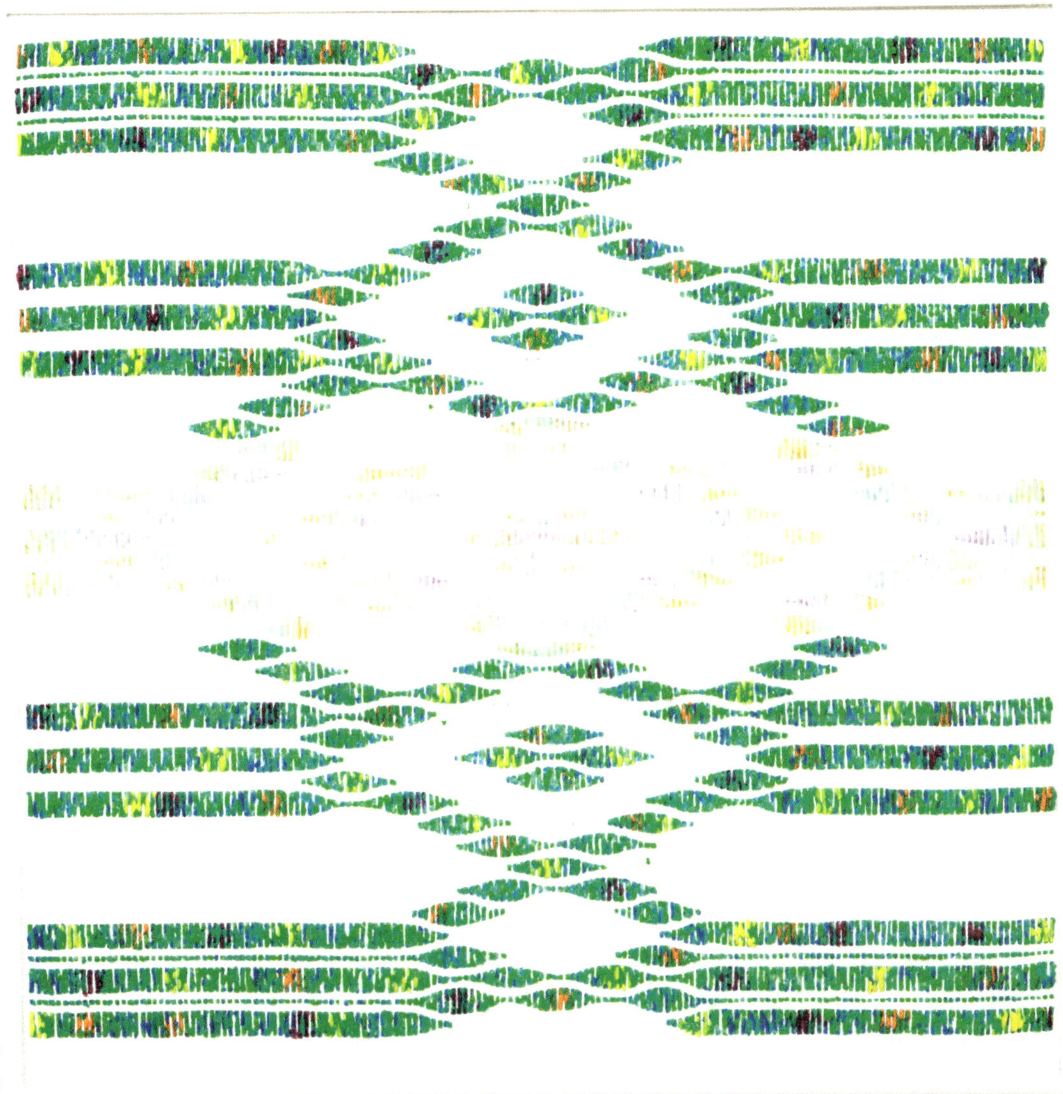

Some days you are confident in your new voice, sure that you can bend words to your meaning. You are the hiker at the front of the group walking through the bush, pushing branches aside to make your way.

Some days you are the hiker behind, slapped in the face by the wet branches that spring back. You are the one who is struggling at the back, the one who feels the burden of the rest of the group's annoyance — forgetting that we all fall behind sometimes.

You blame yourself for this setback and think of it as a lack of focus. Sometimes you chide your lack of goals, your laziness. You envy those other people, the ones who seemed to be always striving forward, but you are blind to their own journey's twists and churns. From far enough away any path can seem straight and true.

This is when you usually give up. You don't admit to it, you pretend to be blind to it — it is a subtle retreat. You allow the busyness and business of life to abrade your attention. The books you bought remain unopened, the lessons seem too far away to attend, it is easier to keep quiet than to join a conversation.

It slips away, ngāhorohoro noa iho. Eventually it seems like you have lost too much ground, that you can never catch up again, hei aha.

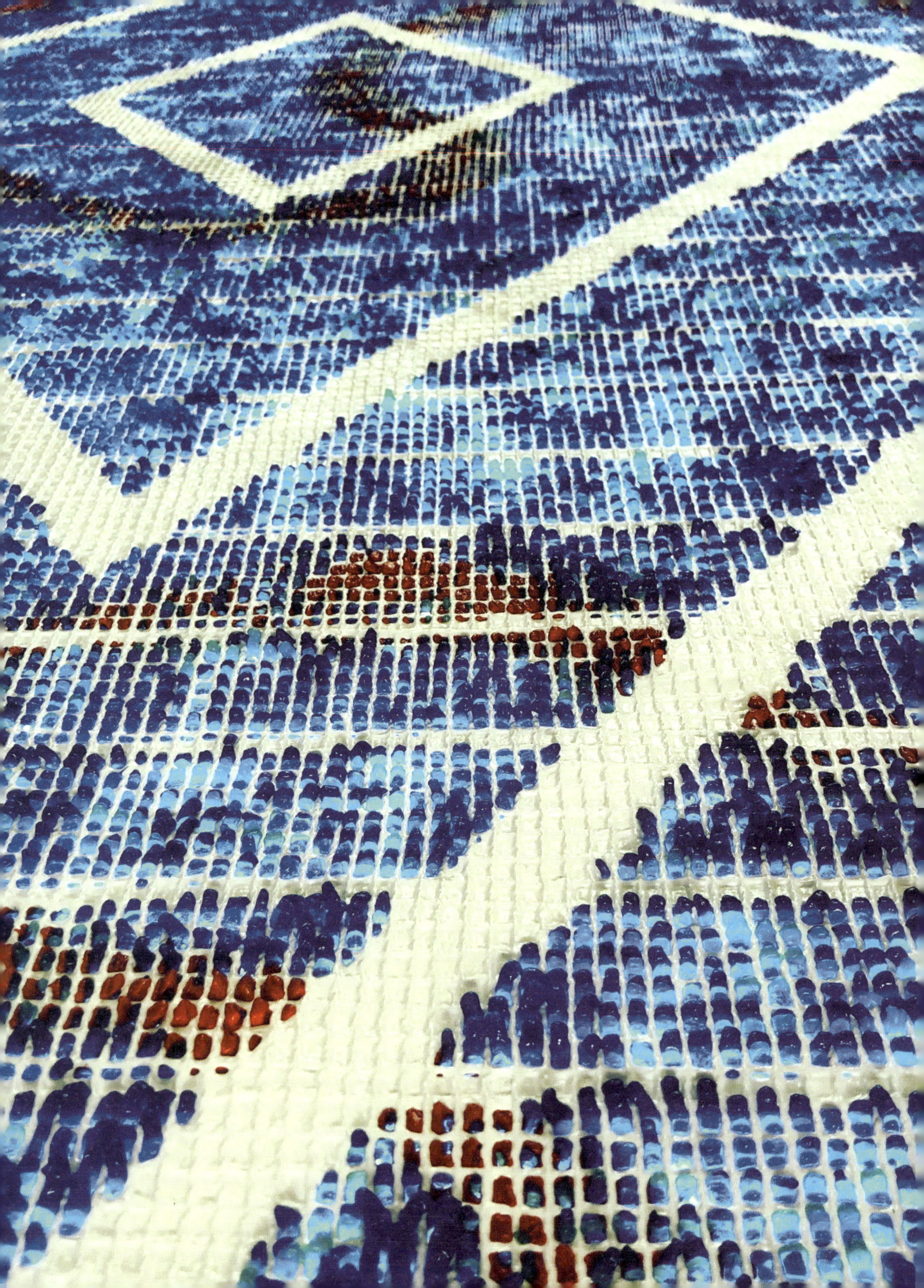

But you have always been tenacious. Or, perhaps more honestly, stubborn. Or if you're admitting the *actual* truth — you're a dog with a *bloody* bone. Maybe if you get this properly between your teeth, you won't let go this time? Even if you can't remember all the kupu, if the tāniko of your speech is knotted and snarled — you haven't forgotten everything.

You know the path back, you know the path forward. This time, as you trace your steps, notice the trail is a little clearer. That your footsteps have cut it deeper. Pay no mind to difficulties beyond your vision — your task now is smaller and more intimate: it is one foot at a time. You don't need to punish yourself anymore for taking a breath. You can rest a while.

Breathe in.

Breathe out.

You will get there when you get there.

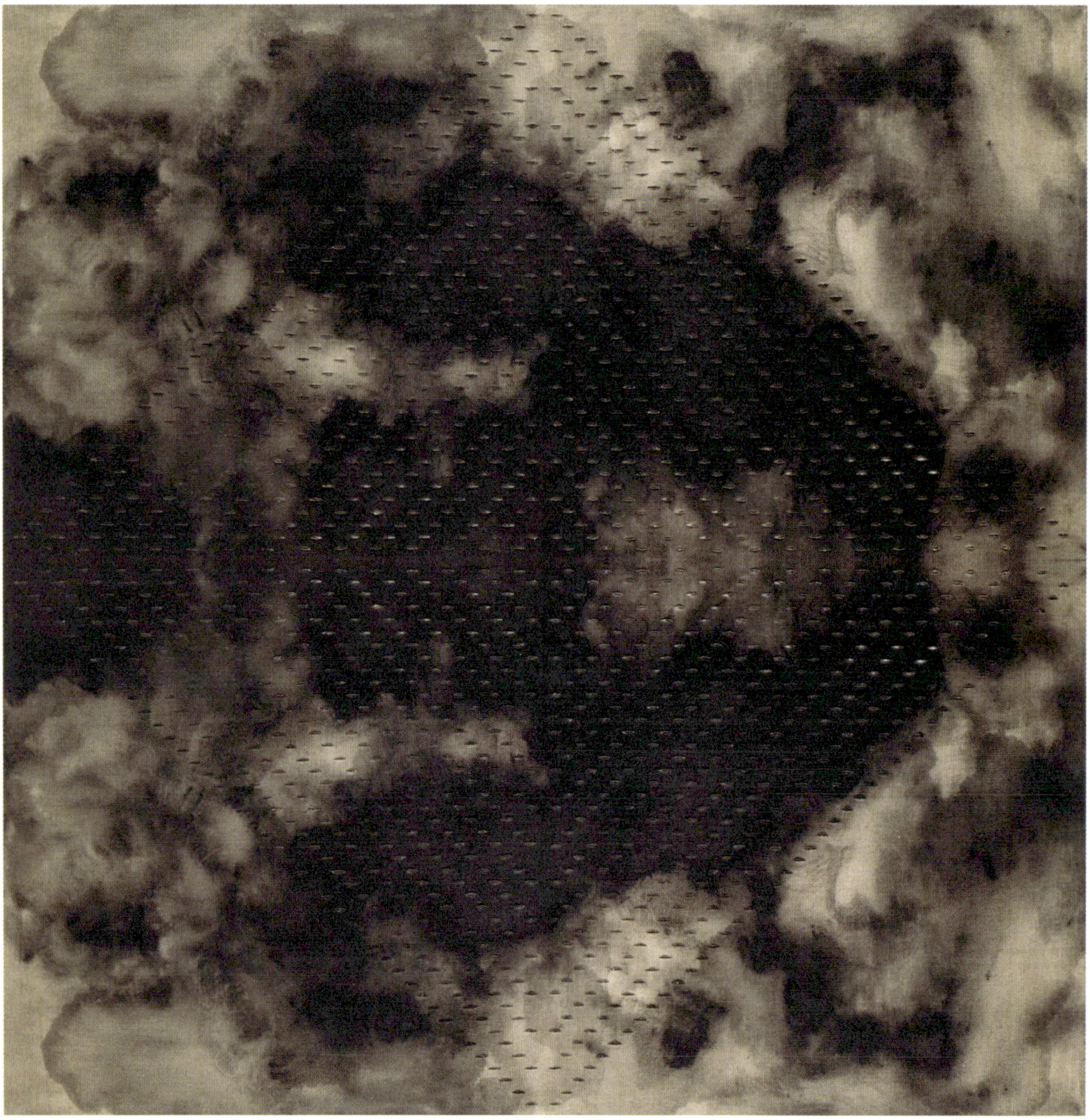

Today you learnt a new metaphor for bird song: te waha o Tāne. The chorus of manu that would once wake the forest. Sometimes you thought that the absence of one voice, your voice, was insignificant, but think of what we have lost since the birds were hunted, their habitat cleared: the voice of a god grew quieter. And we are poorer for it.

You must reclaim your voice before te ngahere is stripped and clear felled. Each voice, each different voice is needed — even one will be missed.

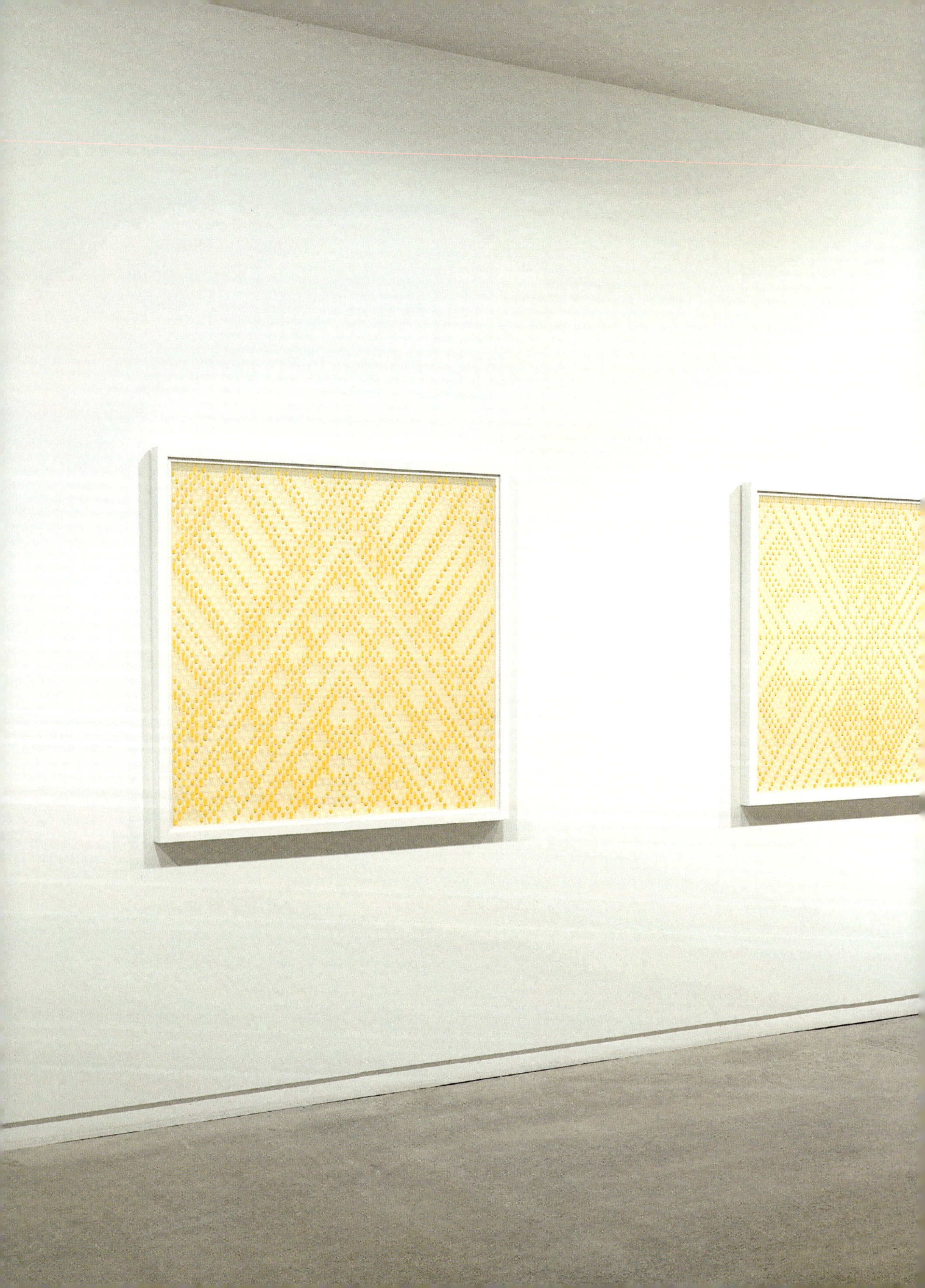

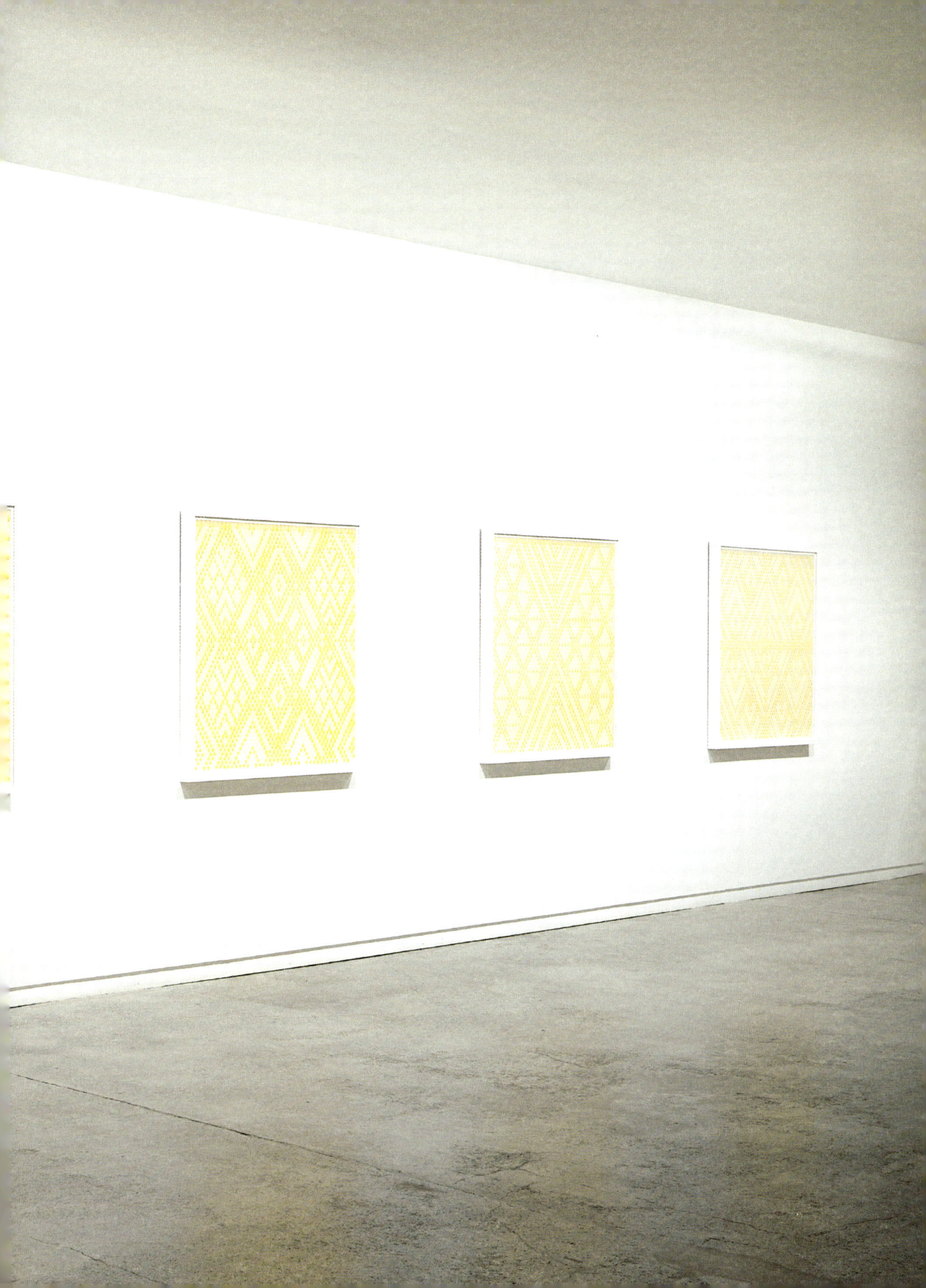

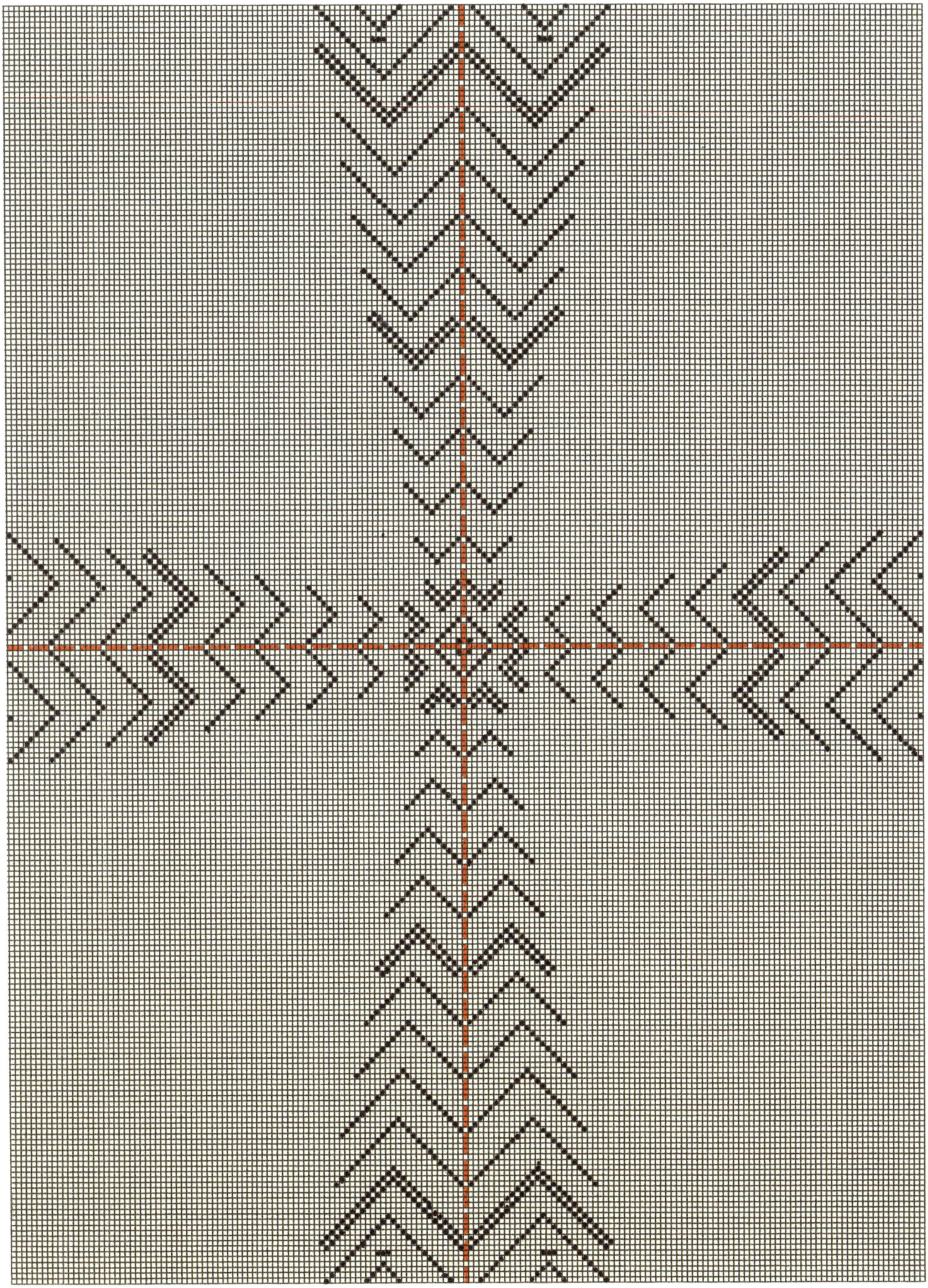

Now you know the shape of your language, you see it everywhere: it is the maunga and roto, it is the birds — their song, yes, but also in the flit and turn of the pīwakawaka, the swoop of the kākā. It makes sense of you and you of it. See yourself anew in its syntax.

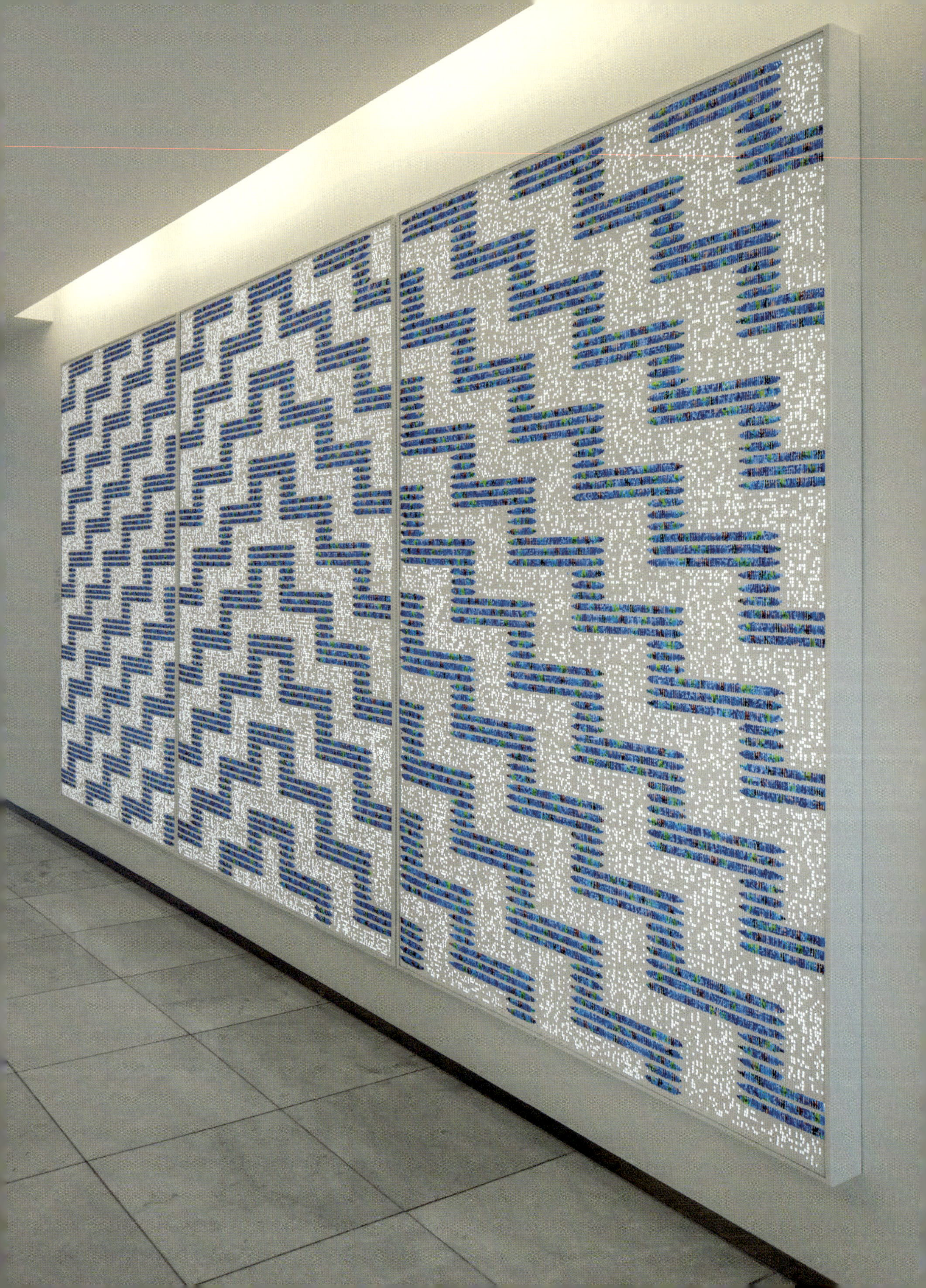

Everything you want to know, all the nuance, the dexterity of expression you crave, could take a lifetime to achieve. There is so much to learn that perhaps you will always be a beginner.

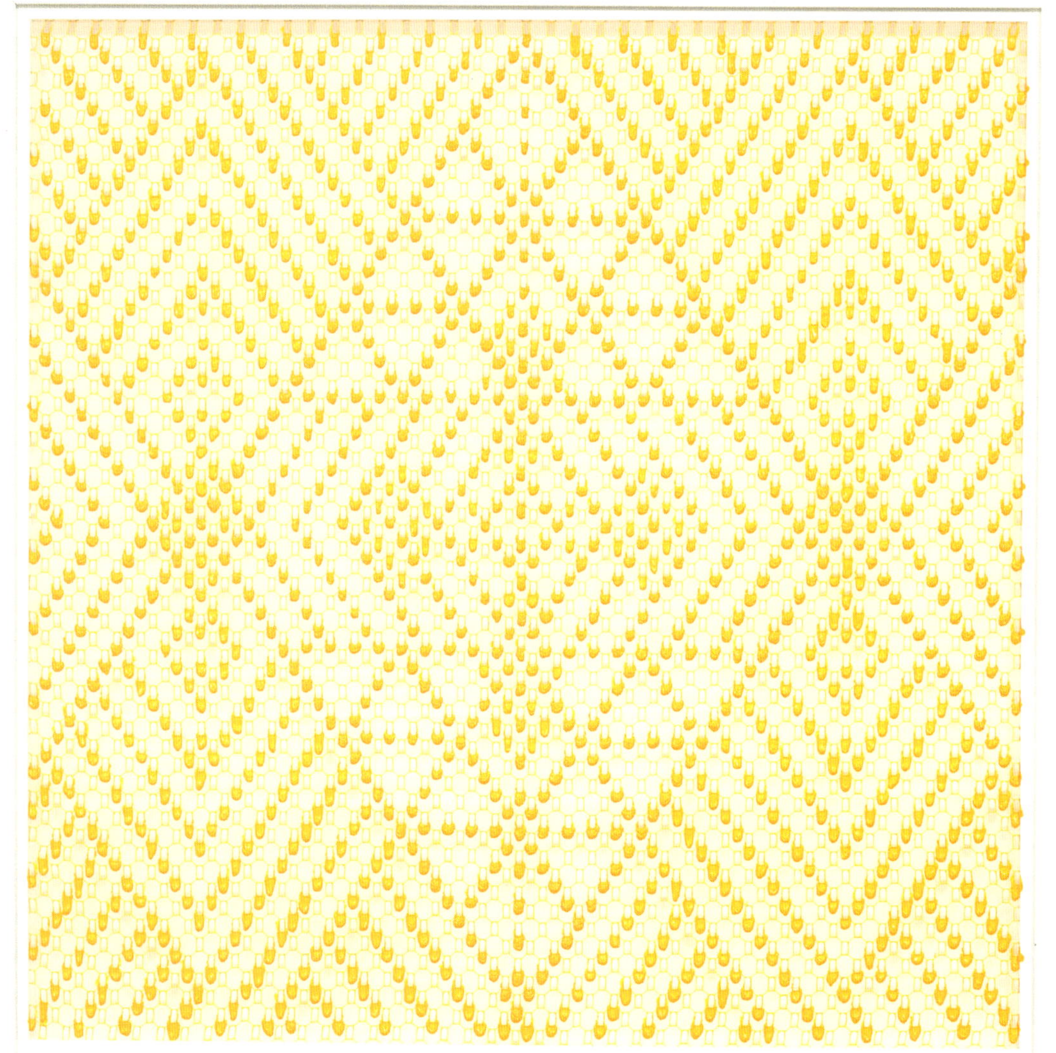

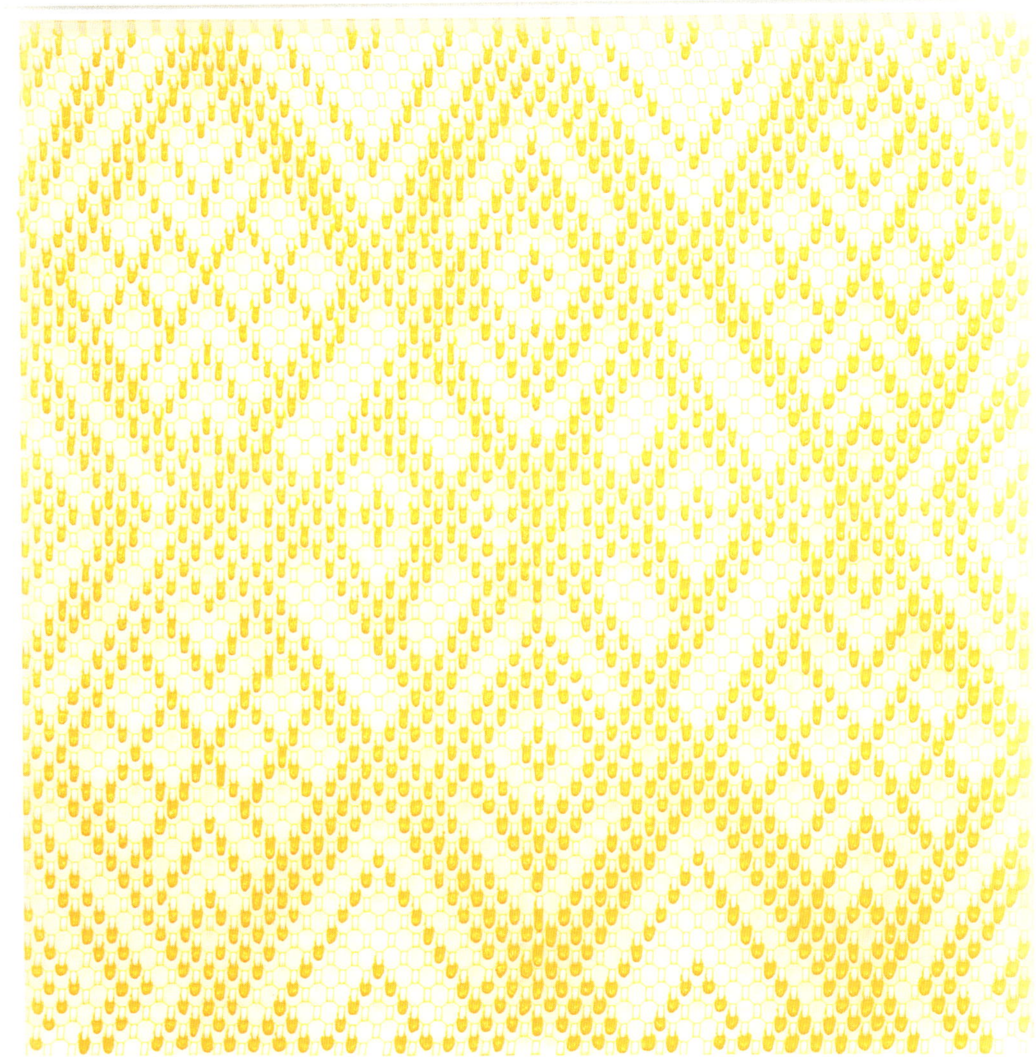

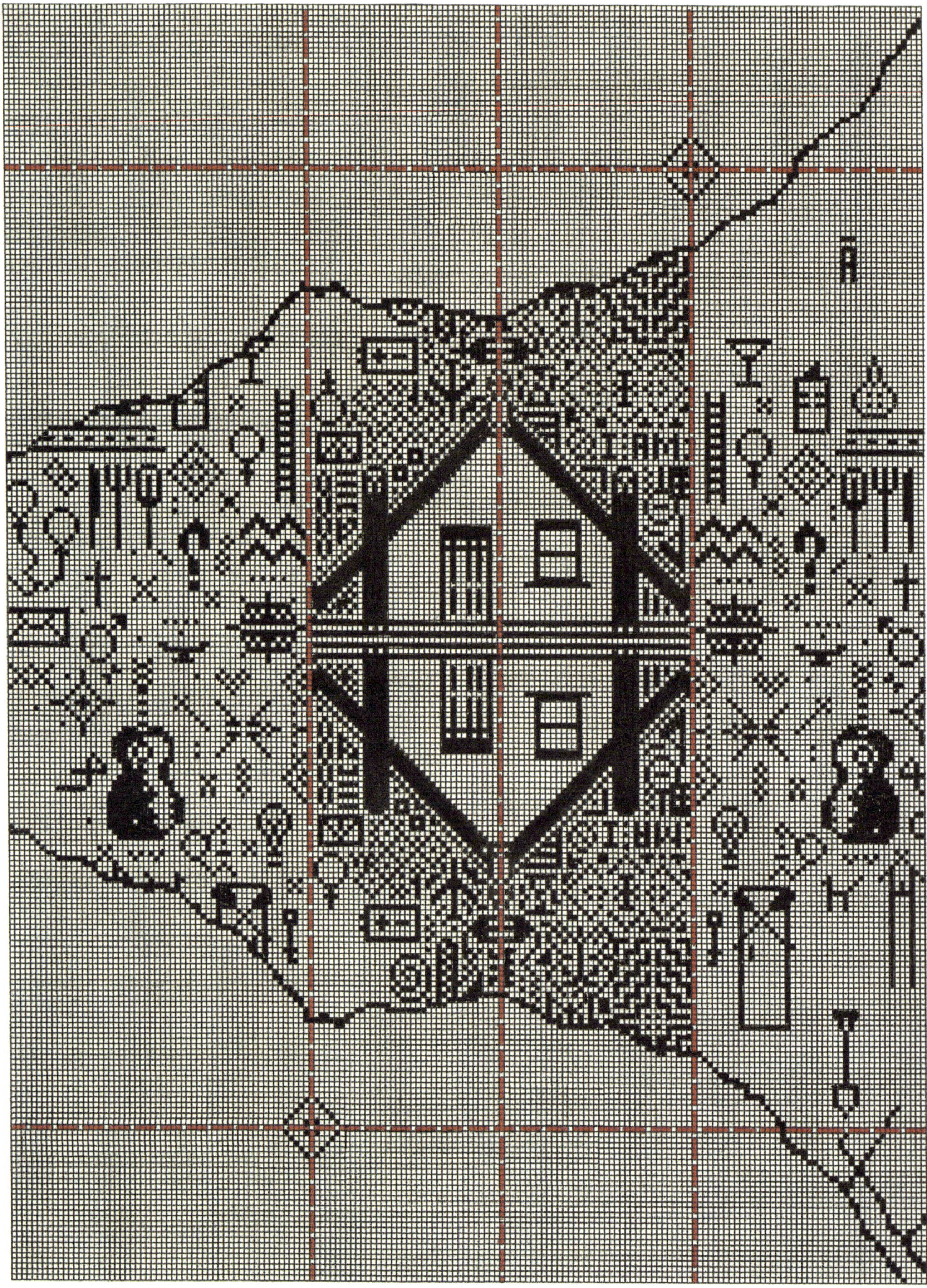

Even if you were as big and deep as this lake, it would be impossible for you to contain it all.

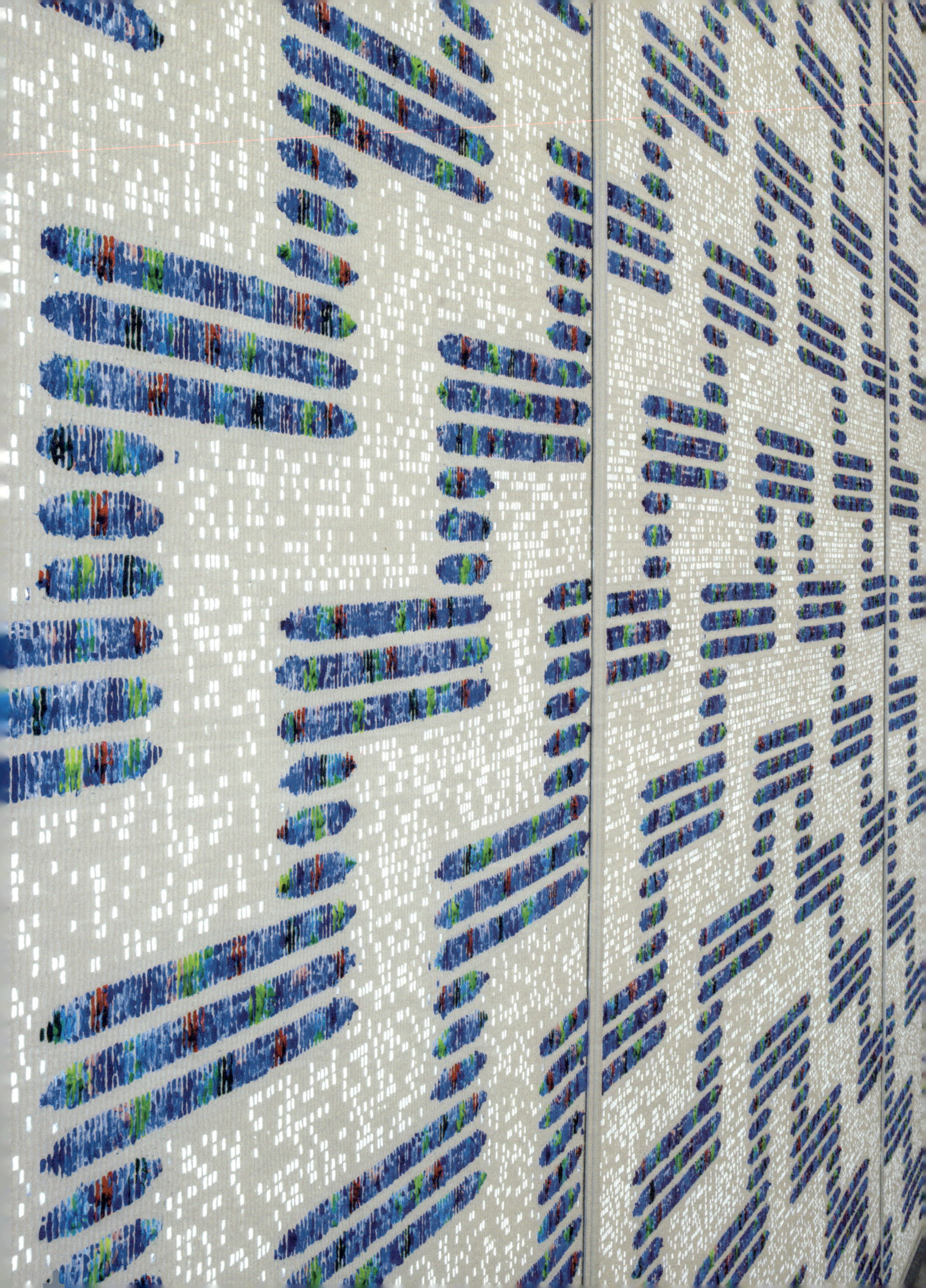

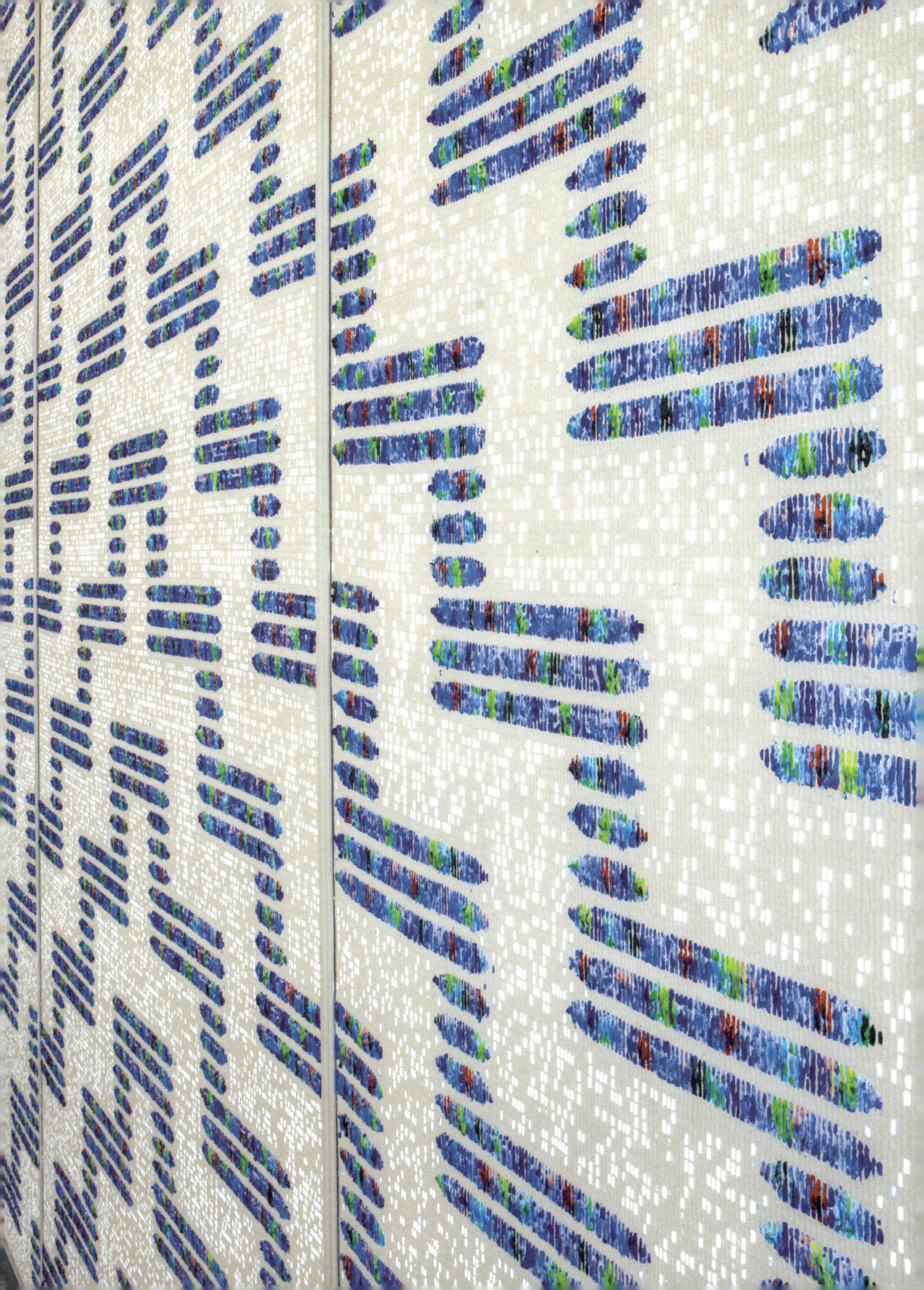

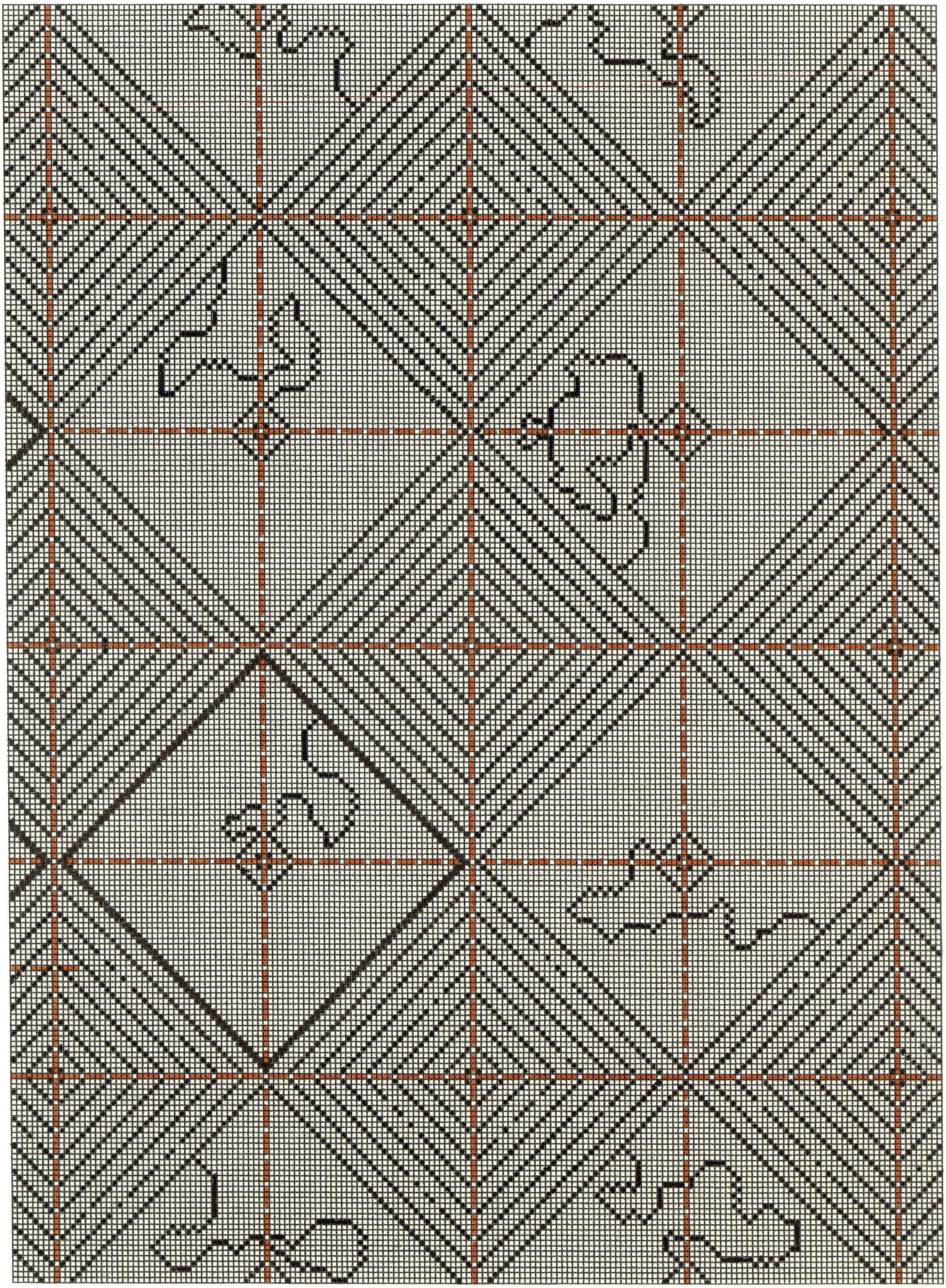

Remember that you are not alone on this journey. Know you never were.

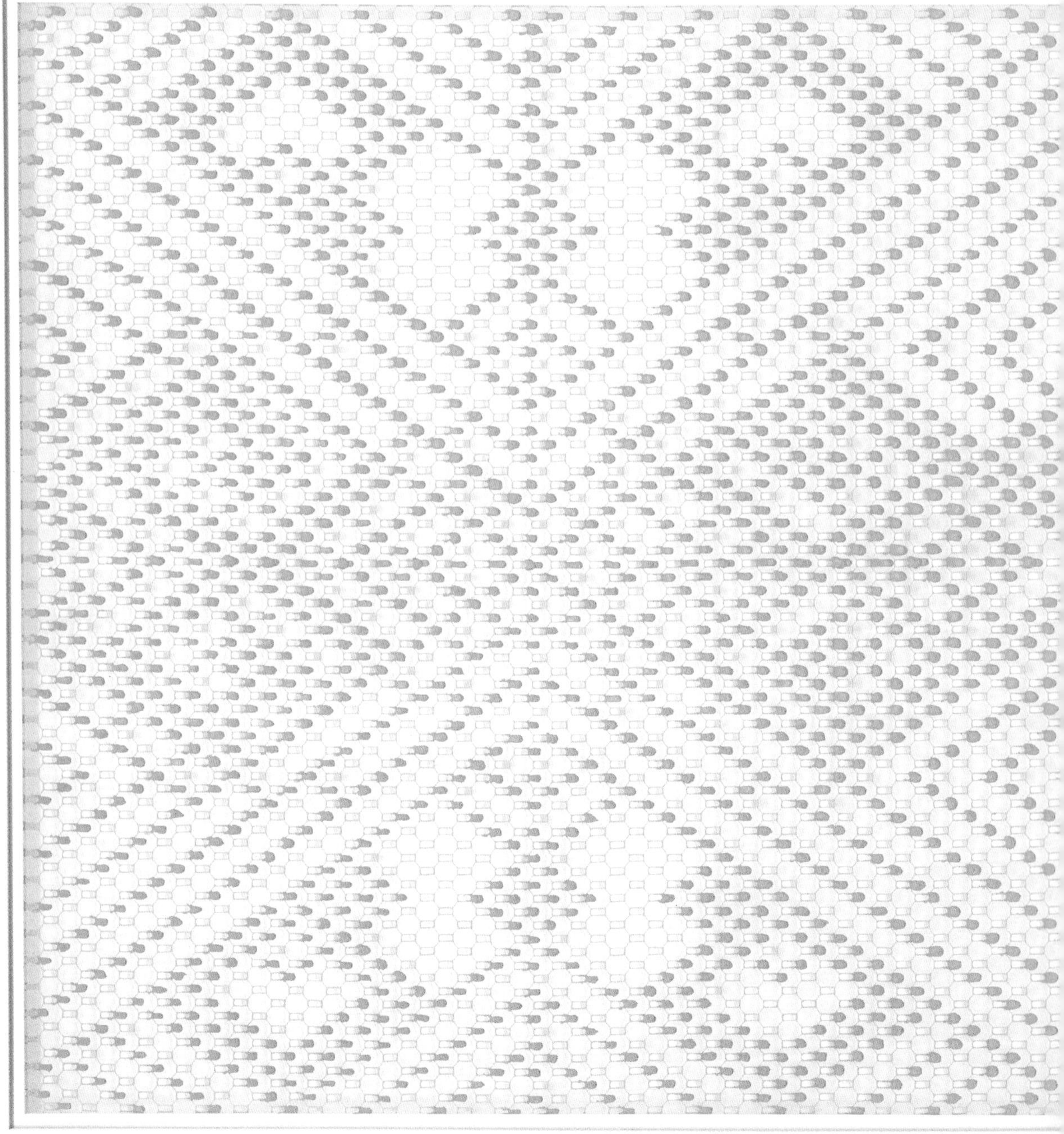

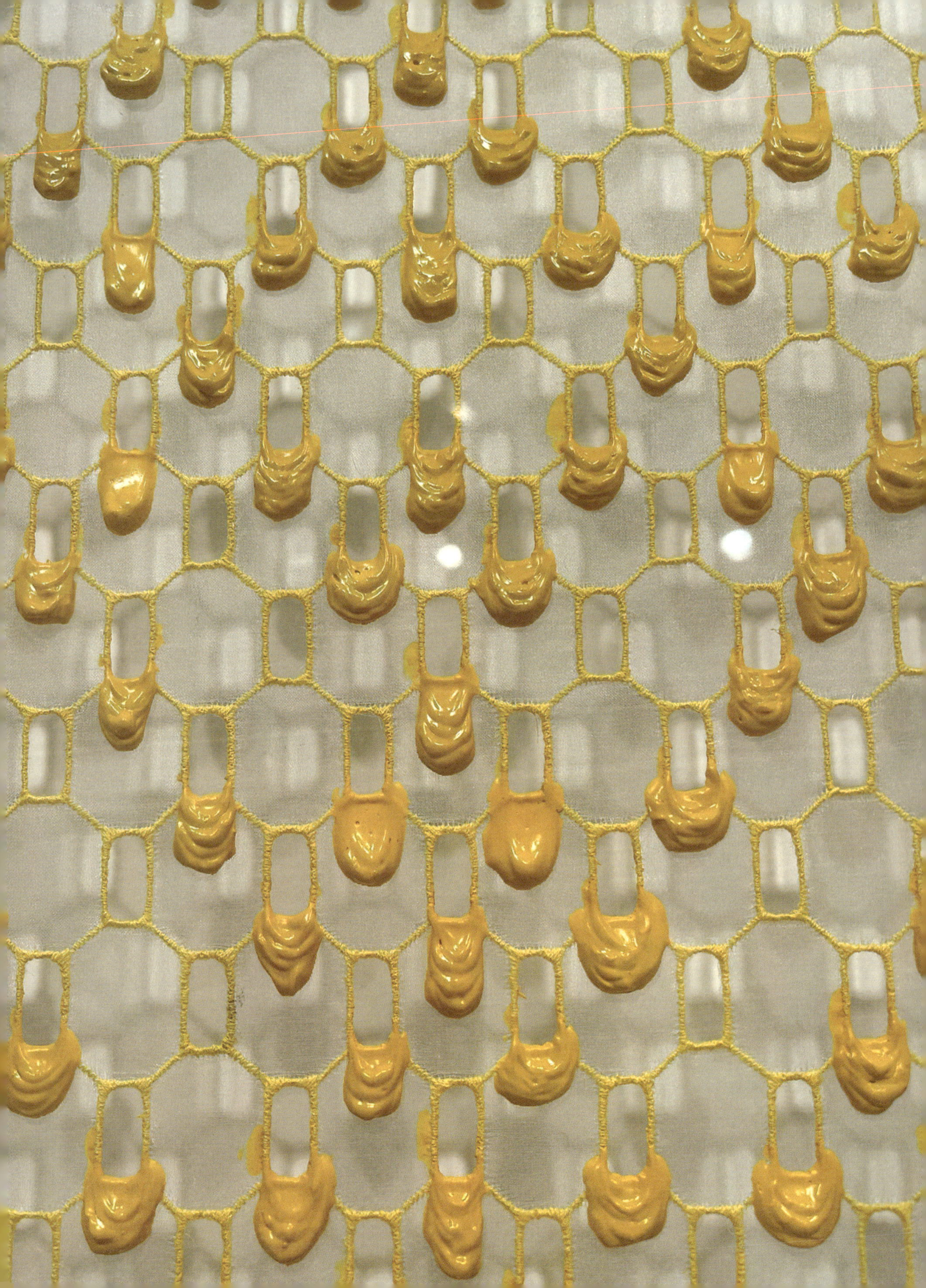

This is the beginning, not where you started.

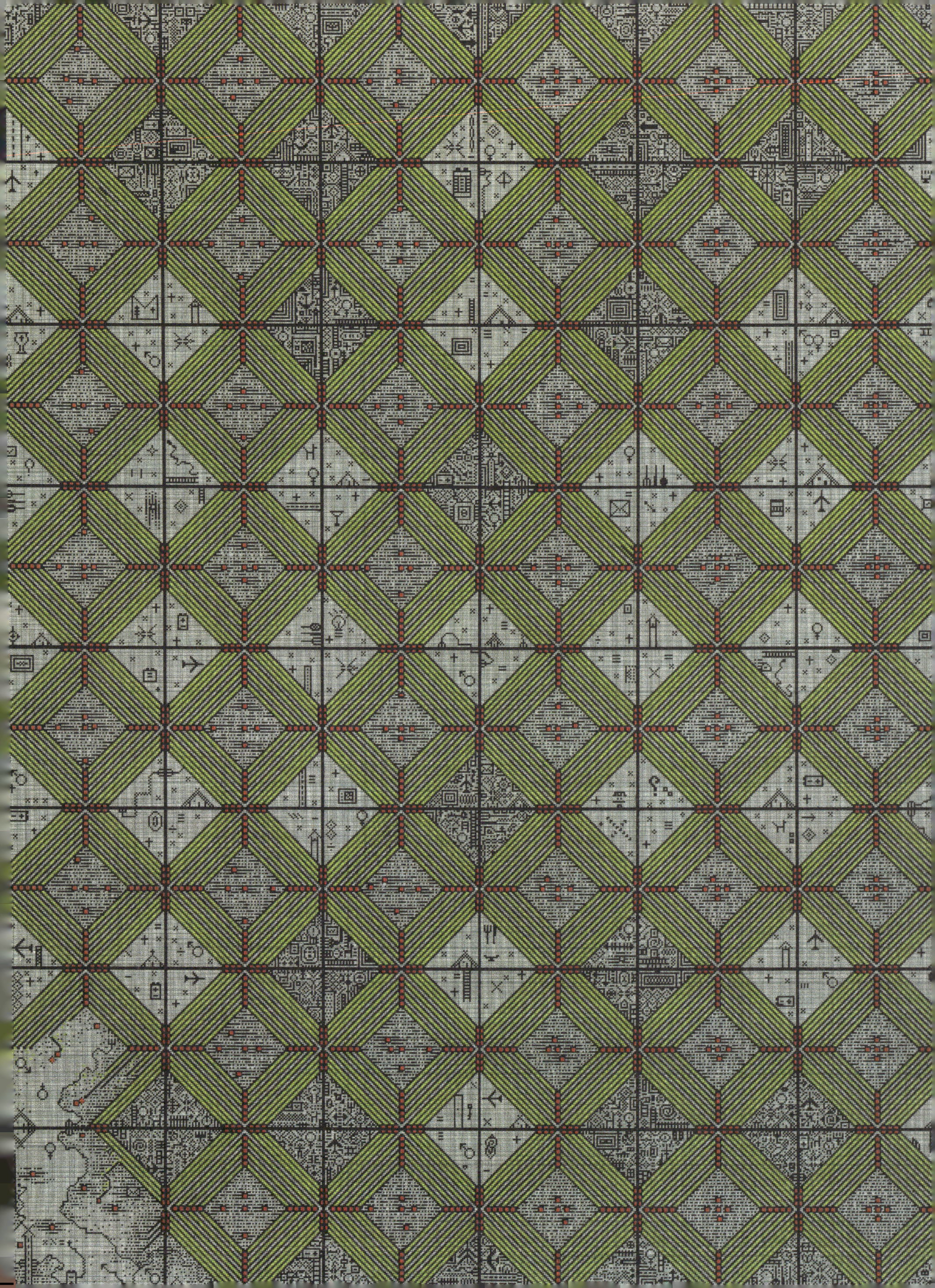

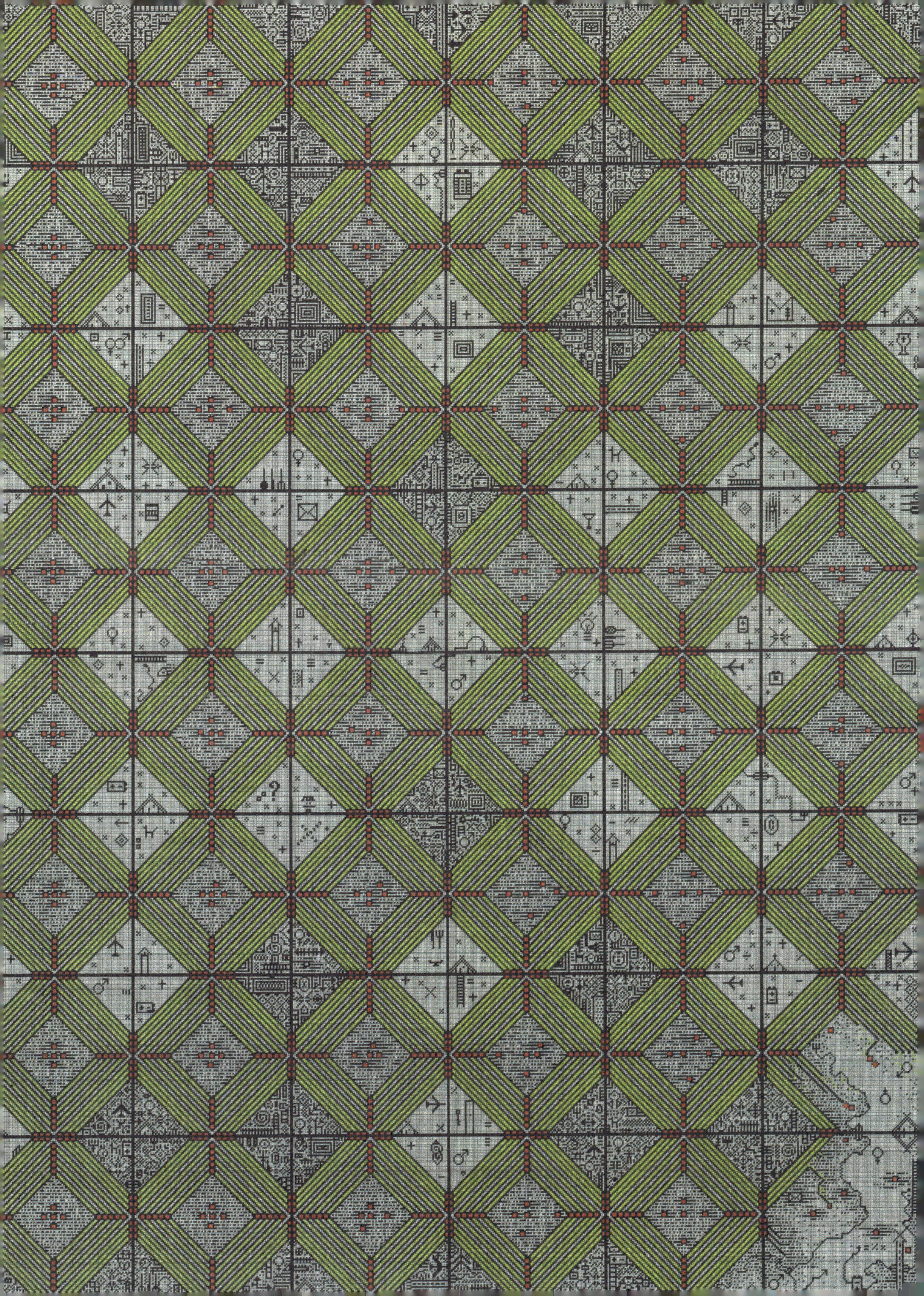

Return to where you belong.

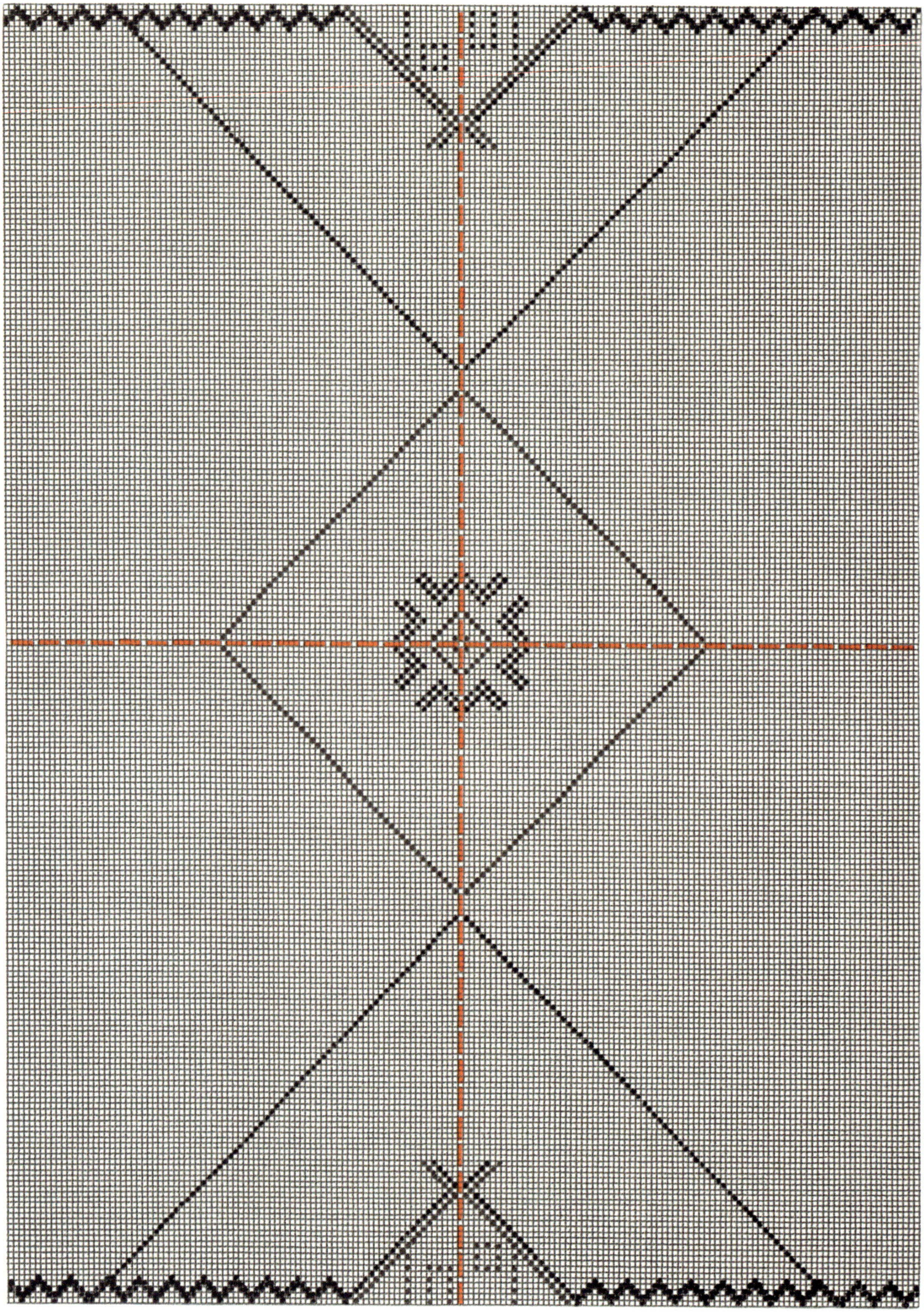

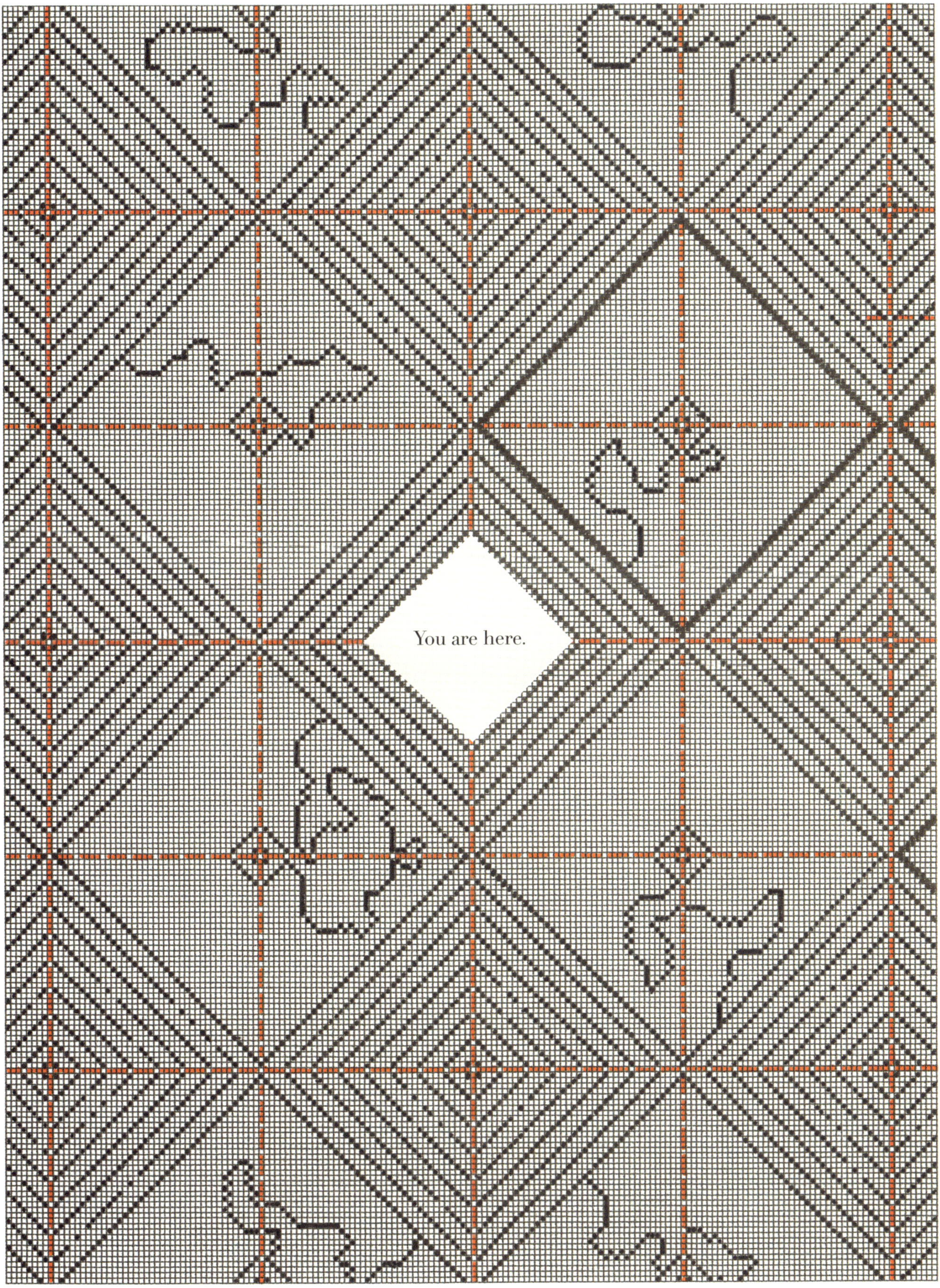
You are here.

Author's note

The text of *You Are Here* is based on the Fibonacci sequence starting at three. The words spiral out to the centre of the book and then spiral back in on themselves. It is my hope that by the time you have walked that path you are now a different reader and will read those words in a new way.

In my work I am interested in how form and structure inform the content of a story — how it plays a part in understanding the meaning. In this collaboration with Peata Larkin, I wanted to make a real connection between her work and mine. As cousins, we share the same whakapapa that is central to this work, but we also wanted to strengthen our artistic ties.

Some of Peata's earlier work was based on DNA and I loved the idea of a double helix — but how to render that in a story? As a teenager I went through a phase of writing stories in spirals, starting in the middle of the page and writing my words in tiny, tight script; that option seemed impractical for this project. I thought of the patterns in tāniko and whakairo, patterns that Peata draws upon, and remembered tracing the shape of the double spiral, te takarangi. A symbol of unfurling, of the connection between knowledge and wairua, of Te Pō emerging from Te Kore. A shape that can be mimicked by forming your thoughts into a group of three words, then five, then eight . . .

Artist's note

My drawing process is to fill in 1mm x 1mm squares with an ink pen. I draw intuitively, filling one square in at a time, creating a blend of abstract and representational imagery on a printed grid that relates to my whakapapa and the journey back to my tīpuna. My illuminated paintings are created using a transparent medium and pure pigments. An LED lightbox tray sits behind the painted surface. The yellow works are acrylic drips of paint on embroidered transparent silk. It was an honour and a beautiful experience collaborating with Whiti as her words describe so eloquently the struggles of finding our way back home to our Māori roots.

About the writer and the artist

Whiti Hereaka (Ngāti Tūwharetoa, Te Arawa) is a playwright, novelist, screenwriter, and barrister and solicitor. She holds a Masters in Creative Writing (Scriptwriting) from the International Institute of Modern Letters, Te Herenga Waka — Victoria University of Wellington, and is a trustee of the Māori Literature Trust. Her fourth novel, *Kurangaituku*, won the Jann Medlicott Acorn Prize for Fiction at the 2022 Ockham New Zealand Book Awards. She is a lecturer in the creative writing programme at Massey University and is working on her PhD in creative writing.

Peata Larkin (Te Arawa, Tūhourangi, Ngāti Whakaue, Ngāti Tūwharetoa) graduated with a Master of Fine Arts from RMIT, Melbourne, in 2008 and has a Bachelor of Fine Arts from the Elam School of Fine Arts, University of Auckland. Her public and private commissions have included ANZ Tower, Westfield Newmarket, Park Hyatt and the International Conference Centre in Auckland. Her work is held in the collections of Memphis Museum of Fine Arts, USA, Rotorua Museum Arts Trust, Pātaka Art + Museum, the University of Waikato and Massey University.

Gary Stewart is an Otago-based designer (The Gas Project) who works in identity, packaging and restaurant design, as well as book publication. He is the designer of all the books in the kōrero series.

You Are Here is the sixth book in the kōrero series. The kōrero project invites new and exciting collaborations for two different kinds of artistic intelligence to work away at a shared topic. Other books in the series are *High Wire* (2020) by Lloyd Jones and Euan Macleod; *Shining Land* (2020) by Paula Morris and Haru Sameshima; *The Lobster's Tale* (2021) by Chris Price and Bruce Foster; *Bordering on Miraculous* (2022) by Lynley Edmeades and Saskia Leek; and *Little Doomsdays* (2023) by Nic Low and Phil Dadson.

MASSEY UNIVERSITY PRESS

First published in 2025 by Massey University Press
Private Bag 102904, North Shore Mail Centre
Auckland 0745, New Zealand
www.masseypress.ac.nz

Design by Gary Stewart, The Gas Project
Cover illustrations by Peata Larkin

A catalogue record for this book is available from the National Library of New Zealand

The assistance of Creative New Zealand is gratefully acknowledged by the publisher

creative nz
ARTS COUNCIL OF NEW ZEALAND TOI AOTEAROA

Printed and bound in China by Everbest Investment Ltd

ISBN: 978-1-99-101679-9